S.O.A.R

Success over Adversity Reigns!

By Abir Mukherjee

USA Address:
100 Vail Road, Apartment – M15,
Parsippany, New Jersey – 07054
Mobile No: +1 9739606874
Email Id: abir.mukherji@gmail.com

FROG BOOKS

First published in India 2015 by Frog Books
An imprint of Leadstart Publishing Pvt Ltd
1 Level, Trade Centre
Bandra Kurla Complex
Bandra (East) Mumbai 400 051 India
Telephone: +91-22-40700804
Fax: +91-22-40700800
Email: info@leadstartcorp.com
www.leadstartcorp.com / www.frogbooks.net

Sales Office:
Unit No.25/26, Building No.A/1,
Near Wadala RTO,
Wadala (East), Mumbai – 400037 India
Phone: +91 22 24046887

US Office:
Axis Corp, 7845 E Oakbrook Circle
Madison, WI 53717 USA

ISBN 978-93-52013-24-1
Book Editor: Cora Bhatia
Design Editor: Mishta Roy
Layout: Logiciels Info Solutions Pvt. Ltd.

Typeset in Book Antiqua
Printed at Dhote Offset Technokrafts Pvt. Ltd., Mumbai

sPrice — India: Rs 125; Elsewhere: US $5

In
Loving memory of my Grandmother
Shephali Hazra

About Author

Abir Mukherjee was born and brought up in Bardhaman, a small town of West Bengal. He is currently based in U.S.A having completed more than 8 years as an IT Professional. He has completed his B.E. in computer science and engineering in 2005 and started working in different software MNCs. 'S.O.A.R' is his second novel. Blackbuck Publication has published his first novel, 'As Life Has No Undo'.

He loves to sketch and write in his spare time. He writes to entertain people, not to teach them how to live life, how to be successful in life or any other philosophical lessons.

Acknowledgements

One page is small enough to write all the names of persons I want to thank.

First, I would like to thank my caring, loving, supportive wife, Shilpi. You are always there to encourage me when times get rough. You are the reason of my living; I love you. And I must say that you are a brilliant plot maker. I would not have any courage to send my book proposal to any publisher without your affectionate touch.

Thanks to my parents and brother, this page is too small to write the reason for thanking you. You guys are rocking. I love you.

Thanks to My editor, Sharanya Bhattacharya – without you the following bunch of papers would not have got the shape of a book.

Thanks to my first publisher, Blackbuck for giving me an opportunity to share my story.

Thanks to all my colleagues, friends, and family. Few names at the top of my mind that encourage me a lot from my family – Ankur (my big bro), Chameli (sis-in-law), my sisters – Diya, Piu and Rimpi and Partha Sarathi Mitra(my uncle).

I would like to thank – Ritesh Gupta (a standalone friend made my survival easy in Chennai), Kartikeya (the man of sparkling ideas), and Dipanjan and Arpita (comes in combo, friend).

Thanks to my present colleagues and friends – Kobid and Jai (my *kamina* but sweet roomies, always ready to help me at any situation), Jana (aka Jango, my friend and guide in official matter), Keshav (a philosopher friend in office), Akilesh (my friendly manager), Mohan and Sandeep (helpful neighbours and colleagues), Rajesh (ex- roomy), Abhishek Sharma, Jayesh (one-stop solution) and Senthil and Rahul (inspiring colleagues).

Thanks to my ex-colleagues and friends – Priya, Kiruba, Raja, and Abhishek Sinha (a friend for fight on any topic).

Thanks to school friends – Pranay, Wasim, Nabendu, and Saikat (the trio, my *chaddi*-friends in combo.) My childhood friends Koushik (aka Sunny), Ashis (aka Papai), Gurusaday and Soumik (aka Pony).

I would like to thank few of my inspiring friends from college – Ritish, Mainak, Sucharita, Snigdha, and Shibkali.

Thanks to my friends from my office in India – Sneha, Parul, Ritesh Kumar, Ashwini, Santhoshi, Divya, Anshuman, Pallavi, and Somasri.

Thanks to my friends from Chennai – Michael, Austin, Shanmugaraja, Vinothkumar, Harikrishnan, Mariappan Kartik, and Hemantha.

Thanks to Leadstart Publishing, who agreed to publish this book, my editor Cora Bhatia, Sr. acquisition editor, Malini Nair, CEO of Leadstart Publishing, Swarup Nanda and book cover designer, Mishta Roy for their contribution in making the book better.

Thanks to those people who hate me, you are my fuel.

And last but the most important, that is you who is holding this book. Thank you for your encouragement.

Contents

The call of jeopardy   11

Rollercoaster of life   15

Surprises are not always good or bad   23

The broken promise   35

Bootstrapping   44

The mirage   55

Every success is followed by a failure   59

Pursuit of desire   71

Relations absorb and ooze pain   82

While dream becomes larger than life   94

A fresh blood scented old wound   101

Rescue Uday   109

Sometimes offence becomes the best defence   118

Hunt for the man behind the drape   123

The quivering ray of hope   131

That magical spark   137

A weird but sweet marriage   143

Whatever happens, happens for the good   150

The call of jeopardy

Adhyayan was shivering under the comforter. That intolerable chillness in the room had busted his sleep. He groped on the bed for his mobile to see the time – the screen showed 2:30 a.m. Five missed calls, few Facebook updates and two voice messages crowded its notification panel. Adhyayan locked the mobile screen and shook it off in disgust. He did not want to be involved in any office work voluntarily at that time. He was sick of his office schedule, 24x7. Circumstances drove him there; he did not want this. It is a fact that compared to the United States; India was inadequate in infrastructure, facilities, and many other perspectives. However, those were irrelevant to Adhyayan, after spending ten months in New Jersey. His instinctive urge to meet Shristi, insane client's demands and a haphazard lifestyle had left him in severe discomfort.

He moved to the refrigerator and poured some wine in a Bordeaux-glass, and wriggled towards the glass door of the balcony. All he could see outside were the streets, trees, window shades, lawns by the streets and parked cars, covered with a white uniform sheet of snow. He was almost under self house arrest, as it was snowing heavily for the last four days, uninterruptedly. Those frequent trips to New York every alternate day, strip clubs, pubs, pizza-parties, or animalistic late night booze parties with his colleagues could not help satiate his itinerant life.

After a couple of refreshing sips of wine, he returned to bed to look at his mobile notifications. Three out of five missed calls were from his boss and the other two from an unknown Indian number, which worried Adhyayan about Shristi, although he was in constant touch with her. He rushed his thumb over the keypad for the voice messages in hope of some trace of that mysterious Indian number. He played them; the first one was from his boss, "Hey Adayan, this is John, there is a highly escalated issue in production, and the development team is working on it. They will move the code very soon. Please check your mail and take care, thank you." Adhyayan grimaced while deleting that. These people did not even bother to pronounce his name correctly, he thought. He played the second one, "Adi, this is Raja here. Come back man ASAP *(As soon as possible)*, I am helpless here! They have arrested Uday. I do not know what to do man. FYI *(For your information)*, they have charged him for something related to that website. Somehow, I managed your number from Shristi. Bye."

The last message left Adhyayan petrified. He took a few seconds to get back to his consciousness and called back that Indian number hurriedly. It got disconnected followed by some beeps. His fingers juddered to find Rajasekaran's saved number from his contact list. Unfortunately, the old number was not functional anymore. He thought of calling Shristi, but refrained himself after a thought about making her panic. He rushed to his laptop, found the earliest flight at 7:05 a.m., from Newark to Bangalore, and booked it. He packed his bags in almost no time, and booked a cab for 4 a.m. He had a wish to gift Shristi something special while returning to India, something unique like her; something he never did even after four years of their marriage. However, he never imagined this kind of situation would arise, while returning to India.

On his way to the airport, Adhyayan noticed a few trucks, spreading rock salt to melt the ice on the road to make it driveable, though that was temporary. In spite of the unrelenting effort of human beings to win over nature, he is left defeated every time by nature. He reached the airport on time. While checking-in his luggage for security check, he received a call from his offshore manager.

"Adi, are you looking into that issue?" His manager quizzed, as soon as he tapped the answer button.

"Which issue?" Adhyayan pretended to be unaware.

"Come on! I believe John had informed you already regarding this issue." The manager panicked.

"Shouldn't it be taken care of by the off-shore at this time?" Adhyayan replied, controlling his frustration.

"But they will leave for the day soon."

It seemed ridiculous to Adhyayan, how his manager was trying to escape dumping all his responsibility on his shoulders. It was only 4 p.m. in India and as per the service level agreement, offshore had to work until 8 p.m. Adhyayan did not want to involve himself in any argument, as his manager knew that fact too; he was deliberate.

"I have to catch a flight to India in another hour due to some emergency. So please try to cover it from off-shore," Adhyayan replied in an apologetic voice.

"How can you take any random decision like that? It's not acceptable at all. It will impact our client and business," the manager snapped back.

"As I told you earlier, it's an emergency situation."

"And I have already informed you, it's not at all acceptable and it will impact negatively upon your performance rating," the manager threatened.

"I am helpless Sir," he hung up the phone.

Adhyayan felt a bit upset while he boarded the flight. His decision could jeopardize his career, and he knew that very well. Still, being in India and standing by Uday was more important to him then the consequences. He texted Shristi, "Baby... I am coming back to you!" and to Rajasekaran, "Don't worry, I am coming," before switching off the mobile on an airhostess's repeated request.

Rollercoaster of life

As the flight departed, tearing off the layers of clouds and kissing the clear sky of dawn, Adhyayan looked through the window reminiscing that day when Uday's 'something' had stepped in to his life.

Adhyayan felt relieved, while he riffled through the status sheet of the current release; all the items were signed-off according to the scheduled time. It meant a lot for him as that was his first release after being the tech-lead. He had to win the client's confidence. The tech-lead prior to him had set the client's expectations very high. It was quite challenging for Adhyayan to keep up to that expectation that too with the same team, where he has worked with, as a team member since the last one year. He had to get the work done by them, without any ego clash.

"Do you have any plan to leave? Do you have any idea, what's the time now? I can't wait for you anymore in this frozen graveyard," Uday's voice distracted Adhyayan's eyes from the grasp of those excel-grids.

"What to do? It's my responsibility to find shit in your codes," Adhyayan teased him.

"Yaa! It is a shitty cycle overall. We will create shit, I mean developers. Then you, testers will test that shit and certify that this shit is good for health. And finally our client will suck up those as delicious food," Uday smirked. Adi had gone through the same discussion with Uday multiple times and was not in a mood to continue it any further. To avoid the discussion, he just smiled.

"No Adi, seriously, they are assholes, playing the same shitty game with their clients and our company is also one of their clients. Hence Mr. Adhyayan Roy, these are interrelated shitty circles, like the Olympic symbol," Uday commented making few circles in the air with his index finger.

"I don't have any problem, as long as I get my salary on time. I just wanted to be financially secured to take care of Shristi, my parents and my kids in the future that's it," Adhyayan shrugged.

"No, *yaar!* We can earn more money, more respect and fame than this, by doing something meaningful... something that we will like to do... something unique and completely out-of-the box that will keep us alive in peoples' mind, even after our death... I want be a known face to the whole of India," Uday said fumbling.

"And what is that something?" Adhyayan enquired.

"I don't know!" Uday sighed, "Let's go home first, I'm feeling really hungry," he said after a few seconds of momentary pause.

Adhyayan had met that exceptionally attractive personality, Uday while Adhyayan moved to Bangalore and joined 'Global Software Solution' last year from Chennai. His trendy attire, tall and slim appearance could lead any girl to fall for him at first sight. Many women of their office floor liked to snoop upon him when he was in their presence, while few of them tried to express their feelings too. Adhyayan felt he could have been a lead model for any Men's product, instead of stinking in an IT company. Uday would act apathetic to that fact. He was always restless to find his that 'unique something.'

It was 12:45 a.m., when Adhyayan returned home and unlocked the door with the spare key after getting no response on ringing the doorbell for a few minutes. He found Shristi, sleeping on the sofa. She looked angelic – soft, calm, and pleasant. Adhyayan felt guilty for punishing Shristi due to his slapdash work schedule. He tried his best to shape his professional life to bring a proper balance in his personal life. However, at the end, every time he ended up prioritizing work over his personal life. Adhyayan bent over her face and kissed her forehead.

"When did you come back? What is the time now?" Shristi murmured.

"Just now! Go to bed, otherwise your neck will pain," Adhyayan instructed, holding her hand to help her get up from the sofa.

"Dinner is served on the table. Let me know if you need me to re-heat it," she said in a sleepy voice.

"No need, it's fine. I am coming,"

Adhyayan returned to the dining table after changing his clothes and splashing a few rounds of water on his already tired face and neck. It was a long and hectic day for him in his office. Shristi was waiting for him at the table and she served him dinner.

"Why one plate, won't you have your dinner?" Adhyayan asked.

"No, I can't eat this late. Keep the plate and bowls in the sink after you finish dinner," Shristi said and approached the bedroom.

"Why didn't you eat? You had returned in the evening, right?" Adhyayan asked, upset.

"You won't understand that," Shristi almost whispered.

"What do you want me to understand? What can I do? It's my job baby. I can't help it. You are an IT professional too. You should know that I don't have any choice," Adhyayan consoled softly.

"Adi, that is my point too. I also work in a private Software Company exactly like you," Shristi retorted wearing a smile that expressed her pain.

"Come on! Please don't start now. I have no more energy left for all this," he requested with a knobby face.

"Same here, please. I never asked for your justifications. I just said, I am not willing to have dinner now," Shristi muttered and rushed to the bedroom.

It had been a long time since their marriage that Adhyayan and Shristi had spent some intimate time together. The first time Adhyayan had seen her was at his cousin-sister's marriage. She was invited there as his sister's best friend and uncle's neighbour. Her stunning appearance in a special Bengali marriage's attire, sense of responsibility in attending the guests, lighting the face with a sweet and pleasant smile, smart hustle-bustle, and witty, humorous ripostes during the nightlong marriage-games had entrenched a seed of love in Adhyayan's heart. He had visited his uncle's house each time on returning home to West Bengal from his workplace, at Chennai, expecting at least one glimpse of Shristi on the roof of the house next door. A year had passed in the same manner, stealing glances at each other. However, he could not convey his feelings to her being daunted at the possibility of rejection. In the following days, they had met at several occasions of family functions and had become acquainted with each other. Shristi's intuition had caught Adhyayan's soft corner for her, but she was not affirmed about his intent.

Shristi had bagged a job in Gurgaon early the next year on completing her engineering and had shifted there. Adhyayan had felt an internal urge to convey his heart out, while he learnt about Shristi's departure on one of his similar visit's to his uncle's house. He had flown to a place as far as Gurgaon and evinced his feeling on a meet with her. Though she had excused herself for some time to think over it initially, her response had turned in unanimity eventually. They had fallen in love and got married. They had planned to switch their jobs in Bangalore.

Shristi had got a job in Bangalore quickly, but Adhyayan had taken more than a year to accomplish that and they had to maintain an isolated conjugal life. After a long while, when they had finally got the chance to live together, Adhyayan's work schedule had turned into an obstacle.

Adhyayan left the dinner untouched on the table and lit a cigarette, reaching the balcony.

*****

A couple of knocks on the door of the washroom diverted Uday's attention. It had been quite while; he had locked himself in the office's restroom and lounged on the chamber pot to watch a science-fiction video on his mobile. He had attempted a few times to watch that video completely in his cubical. However, someone or the other had always reached him with some work. Hence, he found the office bathroom, the best place.

"Yaa, what?" he responded on the third knock.

"Could you please come out? I am waiting for a long time," the knocker answered.

"Why can't you use the other two? I need some more time," Uday hollered.

"They are dirty. I can't use them."

"What can I do? Call the floor cleaners; I don't clean toilets," Uday shouted and resumed the video.

"At least, could you please provide an ETA (*Expected time of arrival*)?" the voice intervened; sounding like a boring office mail to Uday. He came out of the toilet hastily in frustration and found a gallant guy in polished boots and ironed formals. His premature moustache and the sandal-mark on his forehead proclaimed his south-Indian ancestry. Uday felt he would have looked more presentable and younger without that unsuitable moustache. However, he was not in any mood to advice any style tips.

"What's your problem? You want ETA for this, huh!" Uday heeled towards him, shrieking.

It was not difficult for Rajasekaran to be certain that Uday was just passing his time inside the toilet, observing his unwrinkled, perfectly tucked shirt and the running video on his mobile. "See, you were not doing what you are supposed to do inside. *Okaywa*? So, why were you unnecessarily occupying the toilet?" He fumbled to simmer down Uday, nervously.

"What is your name? Which project are you in?" Uday enquired, guessing him to be a soft target by noticing the prompt nervousness on his face.

"Rajasekaran Balasubramaniam. Sir, FYI, I was in the middle of a deliverable, so thought of getting the estimation. I am sorry," he answered in a single breath and almost ran away hurriedly.

*****

After a few days, Uday wondered about finding Rajasekaran in his team meeting. Uday had been looking for Rajasekaran since that incident in the office, miffed at his behaviour. Just after all the participants settled in the meeting room, Uday evinced his awe "Wow! It's good to see some fresh talent in the team." Few droplets wet Rajasekaran's sandal marked forehead, as he was sweating in that chilled meeting room. Uday's intention was clear to him.

"Can we start the meeting with introductions of the new team members?" Uday asked his manager, Shrinivas.

"Sure!" Shrinivas encouraged Uday's proposal.

After a couple of other member's introduction that Uday was not bothered about, Rajasekaran started "Hi everyone, I am

Rajasekaran Balasubramaniam, Anna University 2010 batch pass out and I had joined GSS 8 months ago. I worked in another account for few months; I then joined this account a week ago."

He tried hard to address all the people present there; however, his eyes were glued on Uday's eyes only.

"What is that previous account, you worked on?" Uday darted a question.

"International Health Care System."

"Why did they release you, any performance issue?" Uday probed.

"No, it was my choice."

"So, you have already asked for a release in your eight months of professional career," Rajasekaran tried to say something but Uday continued, not allowing him, "Let me guess, you just escaped from your work pressure and joined this account, taking it to be a cake-walk," Uday smiled in malice.

"No, I didn't like the type of work I was scheduled to do there. They were assigning me on some documentation tasks; collecting other's documents in share-drive from mails and copy-pasting things from here to there. I wanted to do real coding, debugging, fixing, and all that kind of stuff," he answered eloquently.

"I see..." Uday wasn't ready to let him win an argument.

"Let's take that off-line guys; we have to cover several agendas in this meeting, and we have a time-crunch too," Shrinivas interrupted him, realizing Uday's disdain over Rajasekaran.

The main intention of that meeting was to allocate people in different upcoming projects and Uday was responsible for that as the development team lead. He allotted the largest and most complicated project to Rajasekaran, misapplying his position. Rajasekaran had to swallow that unwillingly.

While all adjourned and came out of the meeting room. Uday called Rajasekaran by gesture.

"So Mr. Rajasekaran Balasubramaniam, now I need 'an ETA' from you by EOD (*End of the day*) for your project," Uday mocked, gesturing quotation marks, while he voiced the word 'ETA'.

Surprises are not always good or bad

It was almost midnight when Rajasekaran somehow managed to get some confidence about the project, which had been allotted, to him. He structured a detailed level design for the requirement document, merely apparent from any aspects. Uday was quite aware of the fact that, it was next to impossible for an unacquainted graduate hire like Rajasekaran to manage that complex project. But, Rajasekaran had been progressing slowly but steadily, investing extra hours and effort in the office and had brought the work to the finish line by then. Hence, he was relieved and proud, while riding his bike back home that day. Just before reaching the main road, where the private road of his IT Park finished, he stopped. He overlooked something unusual by the road behind, brood in self-satisfaction. He parked the bike and walked back in hurried steps to that place. Except a human's silhouette, sitting almost toppled over the scooter's handle by head nothing was visible from the distance, where Rajasekaran was standing. It was not surprising to see treacherous drunken people on Bangalore's road, especially on a Friday night. He started returning to his bike, relaxed, ensuring that there was no accident. Suddeniy, his ear picked up a ringtone. He turned back and waited for its owner to pick the phone, but after a few seconds, it stopped. It rang again, while Rajasekaran picked it up from the road, reaching near that dazed person. He picked the call in instinctive reflex.

"*Phone ta keno dorchhis na? Bari firli*?" (Why aren't you receiving the call? Reached home?) A woman shouted in anxiety.

"Hello, who is this?" he asked, hesitatingly, curiously!

"Who are you? Where is my daughter? Is everything alright?" the woman asked, shrieking.

Yes, it was a girl in black shorts and printed vest top; he noticed for the first time. The tattoo on her left upper-arm peeped through her long hair, scattered all over the shoulder, back, and arms.

"Actua...yes... actually, she has gone to take her bike from the parking lot. I'm Raja, her...her friend. I am waiting for her outside. It's late, so she asked me to drop her," he fumbled to manage a reasonable answer.

"Oh! She asked help? I can't believe this."

"Why aunty? What's the problem in that?" he asked, suspecting his mistake in answering.

"I know my daughter very well; it's quite strange that, she asked for help. What is your full name? I have never heard your name before."

Momentarily, he thought of hanging the call up. Why should he waste time to answer an unknown's call for that reckless, crazy, half-naked, drunken, and unknown girl? However, he answered, driven by his fundamental characteristic of decency and innocence, "Rajasekaran Balasubramaniam, *pudu* friend, aunty."

"What friend?"

"I... I mean new friend, we met today only," he stammered.

"Oh, I see. Ask her to call me back in the next fifteen minutes," she ordered before dropping the call.

He lamented for pulling himself in trouble unnecessarily for the second time. He wasn't superstitious, hence denied wearing the ring his mother had arranged from a local astrologer to keep her son away from all jeopardy. However, those incidents – first with Uday and then that girl made him rethink over his decision.

He stood there for a few minutes in quandary, looking for some passersby to get help. However, he didn't find anyone but a few dogs, staring at him surprisingly.

"Hello, I'm Raja. Could you please let me know your address? So that I can drop you," he asked that girl. She didn't reply. He poked her twice. She threw her hands, awkwardly towards him. On the spur of the moment, he got the idea to call the last dialled number from her phone's call history. Fortunately, her mobile wasn't locked by any severe swipe-pattern or pass-code, but a single-swipe in a straight line. He called the number, saved as *'Kutti* roomie.'

"Hi *Kutti*, I'm Raja. You're..."

"WHO THE HELL ARE YOU? HOW DARE YOU CALL ME, KUTTI," Rajasekaran moved the phone few inches away from his ear, as a young girl's voice brawled before he could finish at her loudest speech.

"See, I don't know..." he reattempted.

But again, that girl shouted in the same manner, "I know Sneha told you to call and bug me. Can't you use your brain? How you can call a girl, at this time of night, addressing me as KUTTI."

"SHUT UP!" Rajasekaran screamed back. The girl on the phone became silent, but those dogs started shouting at him. He made them run away, lapidating in frustration.

"Just calm down and listen carefully. FYI...." He described the incident altogether and informed her about their location. He positioned her arms on his shoulder, pulled her out of the scooter holding her waist, lifted her in his arms from the ground, and perched her on the stairs of a nearby shop; she was lighter than he had expected. A beam of light from a lamppost made that portion of the street quite brighter. He held her head on one palm and revealed the face, slowly rearranging the lengthy, scattered hair behind her ears. Her exceptionally fair, soft, and exquisite face with pierced rings at the eyebrows and nose captivated Rajasekaran. He tugged out a handkerchief from his pocket to clean the messed up kohl, lipstick from her face, but kept it back on second thought.

"Hello, are you okay? Can you hear me?" he asked, softly, hesitantly patting on her cheeks, which turned pink instantly. He cautiously rested her head on a stair just above her shoulder and pulled out a water bottle from his bag. He poured some water on his palm and splashed it on her face. She frowned for a moment and opened her eyes partly, but her unconsciousness was not interrupted. He sat by her on the stairs, vulnerably waiting for her roommate. After fifteen minutes, a car arrived there. A girl followed by an elderly man came down and introduced themselves as her roommate and a brother-like person. They took Sneha in the car, lurching.

"BTW (*by the way*), what is the problem in '*kutti*'? Doesn't it mean 'Small'?" Rajasekaran asked while Sneha's roommate came to show her gratitude.

"No, it means bitch," she answered, smouldering.

That brother-like man drove the car, and Sneha's roommate took her scooter. Rajasekaran returned home, confused. Sneha's angelic face had occupied his mind completely. He realized Sneha's phone had remained in his pocket, while her mother called back. He switched the phone off, finding it a better option than answering and tried to sleep. However, he couldn't sleep that night. Each time he closed his eyes and found her face staring back at him. He switched-on Sneha's mobile, called his mobile from that to get her number and switched it off again. He was awake the rest of that night.

*****

The discomforting glumness and eerie stillness accompanied by an intolerable heat inside that dark room made that cute, little lad frightened. He clasped his folded legs on his chest by his arms, cowering in the room's corner. He muttered softly, 'Maa' looking for the only woman he believed in the world. His exploratory, panicky eyes couldn't find anyone in that darkness. He began weeping vulnerably, but gradually stopped, heeding a feeble voice. He stood up slowly holding the wall and prowled erratically towards the voice. After walking for a while in that duskiness, he could see a wooden crate as a beam of light fell on it. His furrowed face lit by in an innocent, undulated smile, recognizing his mother's voice. She was singing his favourite lullaby inside the crate. He reached near it mischievously hopping and humming that song. He opened that wooden giant box with a clanging sound and peeped into it. It was empty and dark inside. All of a sudden, the walls began collapsing apart revealing a scorching light and a few large silhouettes arrived through those broken walls. Their lengthy shadows engulfed that little boy. He stepped back a few yards. One of them wrenched him and slapped him, violently thrusting his soft, tiny body on the floor.

Uday whispered, "No!"

"He had stolen Bunty's toy from the crate!" one of them shouted, supplying a thick stick to the other.

"No! I didn't," Uday muttered.

"Bastard!" The person with the stick shouted and began beating him uncontrollably. Uday woke up shouting and found himself on his bed sweating.

"Fuck youuu!" He screamed at the top of his voice, frustrated at that recurring nightmare. He looked at the words he had written on the ceiling – 'Sleeping is luxury for you. Don't' waste time.' He jumped out off the bed and opened his laptop in search of his unique business plan; time ticked away towards morning. He failed to discover his dream plan as usual.

Saturday morning, the project-manager, Shrinivas summoned Uday in a meeting room, as soon as he reluctantly arrived at office, responding to his manager's emergency call. He smirked looking at the empty office floor; even the security guard's chair outside the floor was empty. On weekdays, a team of security guards used to occupy that chair according to their rotational shifts to check if an employee flashed the ID-card on the sensor and had a sticker on his mobile, blocking every camera's lens or not. Uday used to be indisposed all the time in co-operating with them, as that course of action was quite illogical and fake to him, because of their lethargic monitoring on weekends and absence beyond their shift timings. Anyone can tailgate on those occasions without flashing their ID-card and with a giant video camera.

"Good Morning Uday, we have a meeting at 6 p.m., with the clients, and they want us to take them through our code-design," Shrinivas stated excitedly, sitting on the table in an effort of proving himself fit and energetic. Though, Uday had guessed his intention by his feigning athletic activity, but he never expected that bad.

"But it was supposed to be next week right; we just got the requirements three days back. We have five projects, how can they expect the design so soon," Uday blabbered grimacing.

"Yes I know and it's good for us. Think about it in another way Uday, their expectation is so high on us. It's a classic example of client's confidence and satisfaction. They believe we can do it, and we should concrete that believe," Shrinivas spurred in a woolgathering pair of eyes. Uday felt himself as a member of a human bomb squad, getting a motivational speech from the leader before attacking the target.

"It's not possible in the next few hours. There are total five projects, two of our senior team members are on leave, and this is a weekend. Somehow, we have to buy some time," Uday tried to convince.

"Come on Uday, a team-lead shouldn't talk like that. Okay, not all five, but we have to demonstrate at least one project today in this call. We have no other option," Shrinivas ordered and left the meeting room abruptly.

Uday reached his cubical and thrust his laptop-bag on the desk. Uday had a work strategy to rifle all the unread mails first and reply all of them, seeking his response. However, the circumstance was odd that day. He directly opened the requirement document, which was the easiest as per him out of five, ignoring almost sixty unread mails. He was hesitant to call anyone and assign that insane task on a weekend. In order to increase the work hours, he skipped lunch. The clock ticked away and reached 2 p.m., leaping. Uday could manage only a flawed and incomplete design in that short span of time. Four more hours were left to start that meeting; he crunched on the desk, hiding his face in his arm, traumatized. Uday was embarrassed, thinking of the presumable drastic change in Donna's bonhomie after the meeting. His heart had been galloping the beats from the time he had finished the conversation with his manager.

*****

It was 2:20 p.m., when Rajasekaran woke up. He sent a message to Uday about his leave for Monday, as he had to postpone the visit of his hometown, Chennai. Eventually, he found Sneha's mobile by his pillow switched-off. He switched it on hurriedly and waited for its owner's call.

*****

Uday was in a perplexed state of mind in frustration and tension, and it increased while he saw Rajasekaran's message on his mobile, "I will be OOO (Out of Office) on Monday, as I am leaving for Chennai tonight. I left office very late yesterday. FYI, I have sent you the design document. Please verify and let me know your concerns." Uday deleted the text, bursting in anger. On an impulse of an ill-tempered moment, he opened a new mail copying all the management persons in an intention to escalate Rajasekaran pointing out flaws and errors in his design. But his mind just blew away after opening the document. It was so self-explanatory that with every passing line, he began getting impressed and lastly decided to present that design instead of his.

*****

Suddenly, Sneha's mobile rang while Rajasekaran was busy with his laptop. He was passionate about programming, conversant in ten different programming languages. It had been his source of pocket money since he started pursuing his engineering career, selling the small applications of software, and games that he built, to the local business organizations. Other than a few basic human activities like bathing, eating, sleeping etcetera, he liked to hang out with his grandfather's gifted laptop, developing new applications.

"Hello, this is Raja. May I know who is calling?" he asked, accepting the call.

"Sneha here. When can I get my mobile back? Why did you keep the mobile switched off? I am trying to get you from the morning," a sweet voice, accompanied by a heavy American dialect hollered.

"FYKI (for your kind information), your mother was calling last night to know about your whereabouts. I think I should have told her the entire incident instead of switching the mobile off," Rajasekaran retorted.

"Oops Sorry! I didn't realize that," she apologised. "Can you come near Forum Mall at Koramangala at 7 p.m.?" she requested after a pause for a few moments.

"Okay... NP (No problem)!" They hung the phone up.

*****

Uday dialled the number, mentioned in the meeting invite with Rajasekaran's design at 6 p.m. His manager had joined the call before him.

"Hi Donna, this is Shrinivas and we have Uday to take you through the design," Uday's manager introduced themselves clarifying their plan before Uday could tell anything.

"Hi Shrini! Hello Uday! How are you doing guys?" Donna, their client greeted them.

"Absolutely fine Donna. Hope you are also doing well," Shrinivas said, over sweetened.

"Uday, let's start," Shrinivas, the slavish yes-man to the client ordered.

"Hey Donna, We have prepared one of the design documents. I will be taking you through that today," Uday voiced confident.

"Oh really? That's cool! Could you please share your screen? So, it will be easy for me to understand," Donna said, excitedly.

"Yes, sure! Let me share my screen," Uday shared his screen.

Uday presented Rajasekaran's design and ruled the meeting for the next one hour.

"Excellent! I am very confident about this approach. I just wanted to be sure that we are progressing on the right path. Rest of the four projects we can discuss as per our schedule," Donna expressed her satisfaction, after Uday finished his demonstration.

"Thank you," Uday sighed, thanking Rajasekaran internally.

Uday's drafted escalation mail for Rajasekaran turned into a lengthy appreciation mail. He sent that mail copying all the management personalities and clients before leaving for the day.

*****

Sneha's mobile rang in Rajasekaran's pocket while he was waiting for her at Forum, one of the most-famous shopping malls of Bangalore due to its convenient location and PVR multiplex.

"Where are you?" Rajasekaran asked, glancing over the crowd, gathered at the mall's entry gate and the traffic on the road. Her face, scooter, and ultra modern attire were vivid in his mind. It wasn't difficult for him to find Sneha by her incompatible appearance, standing at another side of the road by her scooter. He reached her, crossing the road and asked, "Sneha?"

"Yes, Sneha! Sneha Bose. And you are Raja?" that blonde, slim and cute girl in short jeans and a white vest top said in an American dialect. Rajasekaran's eyes were glued for a few moments, skimming her from brow to groin. He found her pierced eyebrow, nose, and a long dog-tag pendant of GUCCI, tattoos on her bare neck, arms, and legs interesting. She had long hair, untied and it reached up to her thin waistline and a lighted cigarette, casually held between her fingers.

"Hello Mr, Where are you lost? Haven't you seen any girl in your life before?" Sneha asked, waving her pink palm in front of Rajasekaran's eyes.

"Yes, I...I mean no. Not like you," he fumbled.

"Why, am I looking like an alien? Anyway, I don't care. Where is my mobile?" she asked, stretching out her hand. Rajasekaran noticed her long nails, each painted in different colours, while handing over the mobile.

"Thanks for your help man," she said, keeping the mobile in her bag.

"Are you working in GSS too?" he asked.

"Yes. I work in the BPO (*Business process out sourcing*) department, voice support, on the ground floor. Why any problem?" she questioned back, wearing a guitar printed helmet.

"No, just asked because I never saw you in the office."

"Because you might be sitting on the 2nd, 3rd, or 4th floor," she said and started her scooter.

"How do you know?" he asked enthusiastically, hoping she had noticed him in office.

But her answer made him upset, "Because, all the boring and workaholic people sit on those floors."

He thought of retorting her that 'workaholic is much better than alcoholic', but instead he asked, "BTW, why did you save your roommate's name as bitch?"

"You know what, leave it," she said and paused. "The people whom I love, I like to give them a name as per my wish, in my style. She is my darling," she continued, laughing. He grinned like a moron mesmerized at her laugh.

"Ok Bye. See you later," she said, waving and left.

Rajasekaran was infatuated with Sneha. He returned home, engrossed in her thoughts. He looked for her profile on

Facebook and found it effortlessly. She had more than two thousand profiles in her friend list. Her single relationship status encouraged him. He sent a friend request and spent the entire night waiting for its acceptance. For the first time in his life, he found something more interesting than coding.

The broken promise

Like other weekends, Adhyayan woke up very early that morning too. His philosophy was to wake up early and sleep late during weekends to bask every moment of leisure. However, that day he had thought of doing something, rather than hopping around on the Facebook pages, YouTube videos or TV channels aimlessly. He attempted to relinquish himself from Shristi's embrace, gently.

"Umm!" Shristi mumbled, frowned.

He crept out of his bed, after waiting momentarily for Shristi to be relaxed. He walked to the room's window by the bed and looked through, displacing the curtain at one side. The red yolk like sun peeped over the tall buildings far away. He slid open the window glass and felt goose bumps all over him, while a chilled wind dashed by his bare chest, entered into the room. Shristi shrank, squeezing the blanket to her shoulders. Eventually, the sun proclaimed its prerogative on earth; its bright red, orange, and pink rays brightened the dark sky into blue and violet. The soft beam of light accompanied by its warmth fell on Adhyayan. He tantalized the light coming into the room, moving away from its way abruptly, and it fell on Shristi's face.

"Ufff!" Shristi exclaimed, hiding her face under the blanket.

Adhyayan returned to the bed and crawled under the blanket. He looked at Shristi's innocent and soft face. He kissed her on her forehead, eyelids, and lips.

"Adi, is everything okay, suddenly so much of romance?" Shristi whispered, though she kept her eyes closed.

"Nothing! Why? Can't I kiss my wife?" he asked and kissed her lightly on her breasts.

"Yes, you can. But you never had time for me, so little surprised; I always waited for you," Shristi complained, looking at Adhyayan's eyes. Her big and dreamy eyes released a droplet of tear to glide over her pulpy cheek.

"Baby, that's not true," he wiped the teardrop away. "This weekend we will spend together, promise. Okay, let's plan for a tight, entertaining schedule. What all you will like to do today?" he continued, smiling.

"You decide, let me see how well you know my likings," she quizzed.

"We will go for a long drive now and have our breakfast at a roadside *dhaba*. Then a movie followed by lunch at the Barbeque Nation, Arijit Singh's live concert at Phoenix Market City in the evening and last, a simple dinner at home or we can go for Bhojohori Manna also if our appetite permits. How is it?" he said breathlessly.

"Food and Bollywood, it's your favourite baby. But it's fine; I am happy as long as you accompany me; whatever it is," she sighed and kissed him back on his forehead.

"Okay, get ready, quickly," Adhyayan sounded excited.

*****

It was the third time; Rajasekaran picked up the phone to call Sneha and kept it down. He felt an impulse to meet, talk, and watch her closely without blinking his eyes until tears come out. Those fifteen minutes of her company was vivid in his mind, and he relived those moments several times, remembering every passing second of it. He couldn't concentrate on anything after that. Sneha was like an unsolved mystery; he wanted to solve. An untold secret, he wanted to reveal. He had been trying to gather the courage to call her. Moreover, she had not accepted his friend request on Facebook yet. He picked up his mobile again, selected her number from the call history, and touched the green button. A Bengali caller-tune started playing. His heart skipped a couple of beats, and he disconnected the call, panting.

*****

"Adi, can we have a baby?" Shristi asked, looking emotional, while Adhyayan was busy paying the toll fare at NICE Road, the private-tolled express highway between two major cities of Karnataka – Bangalore and Mysore. They had a plan for a long drive up to Mysore and return, having breakfast somewhere on the road.

"What?" Adhyayan asked absentmindedly, counting the balance he got back from the person at the tollgate.

"Can we have a baby Adi?" she repeated.

"No. Do you think we are mature enough to take care of that little baby? Somehow, we are managing right; we are not capable of taking care of ourselves properly Shristi, spending life on noodles, pasta, pizza, and all. Don't you know our pathetic work schedule," he denied.

"But someday we have to think over it, right Adi," she replied, being upset. The car behind them honked as they had blocked the road for quite some time, busy in their conversation.

"Okay, sorry," Adhyayan shrieked, waving his hand out through the window. After driving the car out of that narrow tollgate, he said, "Agreed baby! But not now, we need to buy a flat first, and you know we have already started saving for that purpose. And at this point of time, it doesn't make any sense to think about that."

Shristi didn't respond. They had breakfast at a roadside *dhaba* and returned to the city for their next plan, movie. One the way Adhyayan got a call.

"Hello, who is this?" he asked.

"Uday, yaar! Come-on dude, you didn't even save my number," Uday asked, irritated.

"I am talking on Bluetooth, driving so. Tell me, what's up?" Adhyayan asked.

"Come to Enigma. I have found my dream project man. I'd like to go for it. It's fresh, unique, interesting and completely out of the box," Uday voiced, extremely excited.

"Nope, today I have plans for only Shristi and me, we will meet tomorrow."

"No way man, I can't keep this in my stomach for that long. Please just come for one hour that's enough," Uday requested.

Shristi gestured to express curiosity, while Adhyayan glanced at her. Adhyayan disconnected the phone promising to meet him after an hour and informed Shristi about his conversation with Uday.

"Can I meet him quickly and come?" Adhyayan asked.

"Adi, you don't need my permission. It was your plan to spend a full day with me, today. Moreover you already promised Uday," Shristi said softly, pretending indifference. Adhyayan was acquainted with the fact that she showed her sulkiness that way. However, he was confident to manage one hour without disturbing the rest of the plan. He dropped Shristi at home, pleaded her to buy tickets for an evening-show, and promised to come back within an hour after meeting Uday.

*****

Uday waved as soon as Adhyayan stepped into Enigma. The two storied bar near the famous Sony World junction in the centre of Bangalore was their favourite place to meet and discuss something with drinks. Often they used to visit that place together over weekends. They had a special seat at the wooden rooftop lounge, partly open to the sky with a designed ceiling decor, which allowed only a faint ray of sun inside.

"Yes! Yes! Yes! I got it," Uday shouted followed by fist cuffs in the air, while Adhyayan came near his table. Adhyayan blinked him to ask him to quieten down, noticing the gazing eyes of two girls on Uday's glitz at the nearest table.

"Okay, tell me what the matter is?" Adhyayan asked, lounging on the artistic, wooden chair as per the theme of the decor.

"One of my old friends called me in the morning and I couldn't attend it, weekend morning so woke up very late today. He left this message after a couple of attempts to reach me. He is from Delhi," Uday said, handing over his mobile to Adhyayan. In the meanwhile, a waiter approached them for an order.

"One plate chicken lollypop, one plate green salad, hmm... a dry *chana-masala*, two large Absolut..." before Uday could complete the order, Adhyayan interrupted, "I won't drink. I have to drive back home then movie, and all."

"Come on my Bengal Tiger, one-or two pegs of vodka can't make any difference for you," Uday spurred. Adhyayan finally gave in on Uday's repetitive insistence, feeling sympathy for that waiter, who was waiting for that drama's demise, grinning.

"Ok, this SMS has one ordinary question, 'I need your favour buddy. I am coming to Bangalore after three months. I have arranged for accommodation and transportation, but I could not find a good school for my kids. There is not much information on the internet. I know you have no background on it as a bachelor. But as you are there, you can visit some of the schools to get some idea.'

"What the hell is so interesting in this?" Adhyayan asked, frustrated, returning the mobile.

"Boss, one sprite, and one Gold Flake King," Uday added while the waiter served their order.

"Adi, what are the main obstacles for a business? Your time starts now, until he brings the sprite," Uday quizzed, as the waiter departed.

"Hmm... I never thought over this matter," after a thoughtful pause Adhyayan continued, "luck and instability."

"Fuck the luck, that's needed everywhere, even in our daily life, job, and personal matters, everywhere. Yes, lack of stability is the fact. So, what is the reason of this unstableness? Think," Uday darted his next question. In the meanwhile, the waiter brought the packet of cigarettes and the bottle of sprite.

"Maybe inconsistency in demand of that business," Adhyayan shrugged.

"Correct," Uday said, pouring the sprite proportionately to the vodka. He pushed one of the two glasses towards Adhyayan.

"Uday, enough of your villainous behaviour, now please tell me clearly," Adhyayan requested, impatiently, lighting a cigarette.

"Business on education doesn't have any season; I mean no inconsistency in demand. Every year a huge number of students are getting admission in schools and it's an infinite loop, never-ending," Uday stated, playing with the glass.

"Do you want to open a school?"

"Not a school, but a website on schools. When I saw that SMS, I thought of replying that, 'I have no idea'. But I couldn't do it because he is my old friend. So I tried a Google search – 'Comparison between Bangalore schools.' A site popped up at the top, containing information only about few big schools with pictures. They had ratings as well tagged with each school but based on some unreliable, handful votes. Other than that site, there were a few blogs that emphasised more on the literature than information, all useless. Though, few schools have their official sites as well, but for advertisement only, to claim that they are the best, not useful for comparison," Uday said breathlessly and continued after a pause of sipping his drink, "So; there is no proper website, which can give you a complete picture."

"So, you want to open a website to rate and recommend the schools. It's a crap idea, why the hell someone will believe on our rating and how will you decide the rating?" Adhyayan asked, mashing the cigarette butt into the ashtray.

"Not exactly, first we have to win Bangalore's faith. Our site will be an interactive and communicative platform for students, parents, and teachers. Parents will be facilitated to track their kid's progress on a daily basis and communicate to any particular teacher about their concern, sitting at home and in the same manner teachers can express their concern to a particular parent about their kids," Uday kept explaining with his increasing excitement.

"But..." Adhyayan had attempted to interrupt, but Uday continued again, stopping him, "Let me finish, then I will come to your doubts and questions. Each student will have a profile with three login accesses; one for the student, one for parents and one for the teacher. There will be different layers of security to share communication, within parents, teachers and students only and public, which can be seen by teachers, parents and students of other schools as well. Hope I answered your question," Uday stopped finally.

"Nope, not at all, my question is still at the initial point. Where is the rating and comparison, based on what someone can choose a school?" Adhyayan asked, beckoning for refilling their empty glasses.

"Yes, now while we are successful to build a group of dedicated visitors on our site, we can open a forum for voting with suggestion only for the parents, the prime consumer of this service. We won't be deciding anything but providing a platform. How is it?" Uday asked, expecting the same beguile like his from Adhyayan.

"Well, so basically, you are imitating the concept of Facebook. And how will the revenue come out of it?" Adhyayan asked, as he had few more things to clarify.

"Obviously from the parents who want to know about the schools and their kid's progress in study. But initially it will be free, just to get people habituated to this," Uday clarified.

"Hmm... interesting, so, what is the next step?"

Uday explained in more details; more questions arose, and more discussions followed for solution. Adhyayan forgot about his promise to Shristi as he brooded into that discussion. He recalled it suddenly while he stepped into the elevator of his apartment; it was 10 p.m. He opened the flat's door with a guilty conscience; it was dark all over.

"Shristi," he called softly. Not getting any response, he staggered to reach the switchboard at the opposite wall and switched the light on, groping. He found her sleeping in the bedroom after searching her in the hall and the kitchen. Shristi woke up hearing random sounds of Adhyayan's fumbles, while lurching in the room.

"You...you were crying?" Adhyayan asked, noticing a dried out watermark on her cheeks.

"Nope," Shristi went to the restroom, answering in monosyllables.

"I am sorry...sorry baby! Tomorrow... Hmmm tomorrow we... you and me only ... will go, definitely; definitely... promise... I swear," Adhyayan stammered, tapping the bathroom's door softly on the knuckles.

"Adi, we will talk about it tomorrow. Anyway, there is no point talking to a drunken person who can't realize anything even in full consciousness," she answered through the closed door.

"Who me... No... No, I am not drunk. Just couple of... couple of pegs; I... I had driven the entire way up to here, home," Adhyayan said, dazed.

"Adi, please go to bed and before that, please brush, you smell like hell,"

Adhyayan crawled into the bed and lost his sense momentarily.

Bootstrapping

Uday and Adhyayan had decided to send formal e-mails to all schools of Bangalore to schedule meetings regarding their proposal. And they went deep into discussing how the content and format should be, at office.

"Uday, can I leave early today and take off tomorrow?" Rajasekaran asked, interrupting their discussion.

Rajasekaran had become one of the favourite team members to Uday after that survival incident in the client's meeting.

"Enjoy! By the way, what is the occasion Sir?" Uday enquired, smiling.

"Tomorrow is my father's birthday and I want to give him a surprise party. So, I would like to start for Chennai tonight, the bus is at 5:00 p.m.," Rajasekaran said, hoping his honesty will buy him the leave.

"I am sorry Raja; we have a lot of things to wrap up by this weekend. I can't allow and what is there so important about your father's birthday," Uday denied, dismaying Rajasekaran.

Rajasekaran was quite confident about his leave to be granted, as in the past few occasions Uday had allowed his time-off undisputedly in some trifling matters. However, Uday's response did not daze Adhyayan, as he had the same kind of reactions in a couple of past occasions, whenever some father related topic had pricked. And every time, Uday conspicuously evaded Adhyayan's curiosity to know the reason of it. However, he didn't like the way that Uday was inflicting his thought on the other.

"Uday, how can you say, it's not important man? He cannot take leave for a project's commitment that's a different story. But sorry, I can't agree with your statement. It's our duty to take care of our fathers, though we never can repay their contribution in our life," Adhyayan retorted, irritated.

"Not always," Uday said in disgust.

"What do you mean?" Adhyayan and Rajasekaran asked in chorus.

"Leave it; I don't want to continue this discussion. Raja, you can take off, but I don't want any kind of escalations on your project. It's your responsibility," Uday admonished and left the place.

Rajasekaran and Adhyayan exchanged glances, clueless. And they returned to their corresponding cubicles.

*****

Rajasekaran had been visiting the first floor of their office building for the past few weeks, but could not see Sneha over there. Most of the Fridays, he had been leaving office late deliberately, hoping he could find besotted Sneha again on the street, somewhere. However, that day Sneha's acceptance of his friend request brought the demise of his longing. He grinned at the mobile screen, seeing the notification – 'Sneha Bose accepted your friend request' like a drone. He hid the screen in his palms and peeked over the people nearby to confirm no one is watching him.

'Hi, 'how are you?' - He pinged her on Facebook messenger.

''F9! Hw r u? J '- An instant response popped up on his mobile screen.

'I am doing good.'- he ran out of words soon. Not finding any excuse to continue that chat, he asked – 'Had lunch?'

'S, it's almost 3 p.m. Why?' – The response came from her side.

'Can we meet if you are in the office?' He typed with a trembling thumb and waited for few moments before pressing the send button. He felt the rapid pounding of his heart and backspaced it.

'???' – popped up from the other side.

'Actually... I was thinking of going for lunch... so asked... if you would like to come,' – He typed to mask his trumpery.

'LOL... No.'

He kept the mobile, regretting his stupidity. The rest of his day was absorbed in different office activities apace. In the evening, while he was in the elevator to take his bike from the basement, he noticed the message from Sneha – 'V can go fr a coffee... if u wnt J'

"Shit! Shit! Shit!" He shouted, drawing everyone's attention in that congested metallic box. He leant his head down to avoid those darting frowned faces.

'Sorry, L I missed your message. Can we meet tomorrow?' He replied as soon as he came out of the elevator. Not getting any response for a few minutes, he started for home. He kept on monitoring his mobile for her reply and slept eventually.

'I m nt cmin to office for 2 days. But if u wnt can join us tonyt @ Glassy, 9:30' – Sneha's message buzzed in the morning.

'Sure I will meet you there' – Rajasekaran replied, impulsively.

'Do u knw, whr it is?'

'No, but I will find it in Google.'

'Smrt ass! :D Bye... wl c u thr' – Sneha responded.

Rajasekaran was bewildered by Sneha's addressing, was that an appreciation or disdain. "Smart ass, huh! ...interesting girl," he muttered smiling and got off the bed for a bath.

*****

Uday reached Adhyayan's desk as he arrived in the office, scrolling the e-mail inbox on his mobile, looking for a reply from any of the schools and said, "Adi, it's not working *yaar*."

"Yes I saw; no one turned up. But I have a lot of work to complete. We will discuss after office, sometime in the evening," Adhyayan replied, taking his laptop out of his bag, hurriedly.

Uday came back to his desk; disturbed by Adhyayan's capitulation and couldn't concentrate on his work. A wild, instinctive motive to meet those school's authorities made him hyper. He realized the fact; he had to invest more time and effort. And till the time he had a full-time engagement in the office, he could never achieve that. He drafted a resignation mail, asking for the further process of separation. He played the cursor over the send button enabling-disabling it for few times and clicked it influenced by an internal urge. He took a deep breath and left his chair to reach Adhyayan.

"Done! All problems solved," he sighed.

"What? How?" Adhyayan asked, indifferently, gluing his eyes on his laptop-screen.

"Just sent a resignation mail," Uday said, cracking his knuckles; relief was vivid on his face.

"What the fuck? Have you lost it completely?" Adhyayan shouted in disbelieve. All their colleagues turned towards them, staring; some of them cackled. Adhyayan looked at them with an apologetic expression.

"What the fuck? Have you lost it completely?" Adhyayan echoed in a low voice this time.

"Adi, two days per week is not enough *yaar*, in fact, one day, Sunday is off. We are losing all the critical five weekdays, while all the schools are fully functional. Only mails won't work. Just think Adi, how many mails, claiming huge prize money, excellent business plans, and all have been dropping in our inbox daily. Have you ever damn cared about them? Our expectation is unrealistic. We know, our plan is the best, but they don't," Uday justified his point of view, leaning close to Adhyayan's face.

"So, you want to meet them physically and what if it fails still?"

"Frankly speaking, to me this job was just a way to sustain myself till I find my dream. Now that I have found it, it has to be a success," Uday said with moist eyes, tightening his jaws.

"But I..." Adhyayan stopped as Uday interrupted, "No, you don't have to quit, just stay with me till the end; I need your help."

*****

Rajasekaran reached 'Glassy,' a lounge and bar amongst a lot of others in Bangalore at exactly thirty minutes past nine. He approached, noticing Sneha, twittering in a tiny group – four girls and six boys. In an attempt to distinguish themselves from others, they disfigured their attire and appearance uniquely, he thought. However, Sneha was looked stunning in that little red infinity dress.

"Hi Snega," he called, reaching nearby them. He basked, discovering one more tattoo – a blue butterfly with complicatedly designed wings on her right shoulder's back.

"It's Sneha," she tilted her face close to his ears and whispered. The fragrance of her perfume was tantalizing. She moved away and started introducing her group loudly, "Hi friends; this is Raja, our new friend. And Raja, this is Garima, this is Rohit ....." However, the lingering scent of her perfume was still there on his shoulder and ear; he breathed in it, listening inattentively to their names.

"Where you found this clown?" one of her friends said, giggling.

"Come on, don't do it. He is my guest. How mean you are!' Sneha burst in anger.

"Sneha, look at him, as if he has come for some interview directly from some temple. Look at his striped-shirt and bell-bottom trouser, it's hilarious," another guy taunted followed by a high-five with the previous guy, cackling.

Sneha showed them her middle finger and tugged Rajasekaran, holding his hand out of that place. Few of her friends, especially the girls, tried to cool her down, but she did not stop until they reached the place where Rajasekaran had parked his bike.

"Raja, please take me somewhere out of here. I can't tolerate these assholes," Sneha said, weeping.

Rajasekaran flew her away from that place before she could change her mind. Sneha perched her head on his shoulder. He felt her tears soaking his shirt slowly.

"BTW, where do you want to go?" he asked, after fifteen minutes of driving around.

"I don't know," Sneha muttered.

"Shall I drop ...," He paused, realizing he was about to spoil an opportunity to spend time with her.

Other than restaurants, there was no place to head for them at that point of time. The handful of lakes and parks, which could rescue their existence from the large encroachment of urban infrastructure of the city, used to close before eight in the evening. They dropped by at a multi-cuisine restaurant for dinner.

"I am sorry Raja. I shouldn't have called you," Sneha apologised after they occupied a table.

"FYI, you shouldn't be, it's not at all your fault," he consoled, taking the menu-card from the waiter. "Now cheer up and tell me what you want to have tonight ASAP," he held the menu-card in front of her face.

"Whatever you like, I am not in the mood," she said, pushing the card away, frowning.

"Why are you so upset? I didn't mind anything,"

"I fought with my old friends and I might lose them. They won't talk to me anymore," she droned on.

"Lesson learnt, if they are so important, you shouldn't have a fight with them for me, about whom you hardly know about,"

"Hello, don't give me all that philosophical shit! Okay? They did wrong, and I wanted to correct them. I didn't fight for you. I hope they will realize that fact," she brawled.

"If they are your true friends, they will; don't worry."

After the dinner, Rajasekaran dropped her at her PG. She got down from the bike and approached the staircase.

"To... morrow?" he fumbled from behind.

She came back near him and said, "Yes, Saturday. So?"

"Can we meet..." he stammered, looking at Sneha staring at him, "No, I... I mean, if possible," he completed somehow.

"No! What do you think, I was dating you? I was upset today, so I didn't care," she snapped back.

Instead of discouraging, Sneha's words spurred him to riposte, "Okay, then call me when you will be upset again. I know everyone will be with you in happy and good moments." A pleasant smile evidently appeared on her face.

"Bye Snega." Rajasekaran vanished in the darkness, leaving the smoky trace behind out of his bike. Sneha stood there for a few moments, gazed, and went inside her PG.

"Darling, please don't make any noise, just go to your bed and sleep," Sneha's roommate bespoke, pushing her to the bed by her shoulder as if she is a kid.

"What happened? Why are you trying to be my grandmother?" Sneha asked.

"Today, the PG-owner came to collect the rent. The girls from the next room complained to him about you, and he warned me, he would kick you out if you further make any noise at night," she blabbered, panting.

"I am not drunk," she said, shaking her shoulder off from her grip and went to change her dress.

"Wow!! How did that happen, out of money? No, in that case your spoilt friends would have lent you money, bunch of assholes," she self analyzed, shocked.

"I fought with them," Sneha informed and walked into the restroom.

"That's great. Please, come out of the group Sneha. Look at you sweetheart; you are like an innocent angel. Why the hell are you spoiling your life? They aren't good for you; believe me. Think about your career, life. Do something constructive. Why don't you start your singing classes again?" she continued standing at the closed bathroom's door.

"Good night darling!" Sneha replied from inside.

"Okay, good night. Do whatever you want," she said at a louder pitch so that Sneha could hear, switching off the light.

Sneha came out and tossed herself on the bed. Her disappointment was replaced by a pleasing exhilaration. After quite a long while, she had spent a refreshing, calm evening away from the crowd of the pub, loud music, alcohol and her boisterous friends. She basked thinking, how that stranger guy had absorbed all her disheartenment of the early evening; he might not be up to date in adaptation of modern attire, but smarter than her and her friends in psyche, an awesome listener, who tolerated her insane sulkiness throughout the evening. A smile appeared on her face, thinking of his weird talking manner of using abbreviations and phrases in official mails; still he conveyed his heart out saying – 'call me when you will be upset again. I know everyone will be with you in your happy and good moments.' She pulled the pillow and held it tightly in her arms flipping the side. She whispered, "Snega!" and giggled.

"What's the matter?" her roommate blabbered in a sleepy voice, annoyed.

"How should my life partner be, according to you?" Sneha whispered, turning the bedside lamp on.

"Calm, composed and a brave hearted person, who can control an unexpected, crazy girl like you," she said in a sleepy voice.

"Even if he couldn't pronounce my name properly and talks as if he is reading out mails?" Sneha asked.

"What rubbish?"

"Nothing!" Sneha giggled and switched the light off.

*****

"So, how is life Uday?" Shrinivas asked wearing an overwhelmed smile, as if he had gotten a lifetime opportunity to speak with his celebrity-crush since his puberty.

"Absolutely fine! In fact, I have just found the way to live my life, on my own terms," Uday replied pleasantly, judging his manager's intention to call him in his cabin on the next day of his resignation. In his eight years of IT experience, he had learnt to suspect a manager's geniality, as that cannot be driven by altruism.

"That nice! I appreciate your attitude," Shrinivas said in a loud and pseudo-lofty voice; pouring hot water in a cup. "Uday, have you observed, this cup is actually worthless if you don't keep it straight on a flat surface. Because if you tilt it to any side, water will spill over," he continued, tugging a teabag from a packet.

He dipped the teabag in to the cup and added after a pause, "Hence, everyone will throw this cup, if it can't stay in equilibrium. Do you like to have tea by the way?"

"No thanks, I prefer coffee," Uday refused.

"Hmm. This equilibrium theory is true for a coffee mug as well," Shrinivas commented, cherishing a sip of the tea.

"But your theory is incomplete Shrinivas, applicable for those who serve the tea, but to drink it one has to tilt the cup or mug," Uday retorted and continued sighing, "I am not in mood to serve anymore. I want to drink!"

"I see! So, where are you up to, business?" Shrinivas asked directly this time.

"Yes! And I need more time for that. I can't work in office half-heartedly as that's not my characteristic."

"May I know the business you are planning for?" Shrinivas asked and before Uday could utter anything, he continued implementing his managerial skill, honed in several corporate trainings, "Leave all that. Do you have any idea what the company is planning for you?"

"I am not interested. That's their dream; it's mine," Uday condemned in short.

"Don't be so pre-occupied; first listen then decide." Shrinivas commanded, concealing his anger under a fake smile. Uday quietened allowing him to finish.

"We are planning to give you the golden opportunity to work with clients directly at on-shore. I have already proposed your name for H1B," Shrinivas attempted to entice Uday by the ultimate temptation, he could provide. Uday nodded in disagreement.

"Fine dude! Then there is nothing to discuss anymore. I will approve your separation," Shrinivas said in his original impolite idiom this time and turned his face towards his laptop.

"By the way, I will schedule a series of meetings for the KT (knowledge transfer) sessions. Anyway, you still have to stay here for the next four months," Shrinivas informed, while Uday approached to the exit leaving the chair.

"Why four months? Is it not three?" Uday questioned agitatedly returning to the table.

"Yup! That's general time period, but that can be modified according to the requirement and in some special cases," Shrinivas replied, removing his corporate mask.

Uday leaned his face close to him keeping his hands on the table and whispered, "I can complete all my KT sessions in two weeks and I am not any special case. Don't mess with me; I can abscond otherwise, as I don't need your relief letter."

Uday left the room banging the door.

The mirage

Adhyayan's reminiscence was interrupted by the landing announcement of the flight. He buckled the seatbelt, straightened his seat, and waited early for the flight's wheel to touch the ground of his very own Bengaluru.

The Kempegowda International airport; it had got a new name like the city, Bengaluru. Adhyayan had been in Kolkata and Chennai, before he had shifted to Bangalore; but those cities had failed to impress him the way this city had. He used to feel a strange comfort here. He liked to ignore its high cost of living and heavy traffic jams for its pleasurable weather throughout the year. And the most-impressive attribute of this city to him, was that it was a true cosmopolitan, not only in census but by the spirit of its people.

Shristi waved as soon as Adhyayan appeared at the exit of the arrival terminal. Adhyayan ran to her and hugged her, lifting her from the ground.

"How are you?" Shristi asked; her eyes moist yet smiling.

"Rocking, now!" Adhyayan exclaimed and attempted to kiss her.

"This is India and a public place too. So, please put me down; everyone is staring at us," Shristi said, placing her palm on his mouth. Adhyayan released her, noticing many frowning faces, gazing at them.

"*Oye* Hero! Take your trolley, if your scene is over," a policeman shouted. They collected the handcart and left the place abruptly, embarrassed.

"I will drive," Adhyayan demanded while they reached their car at the parking. Two years ago, Adhyayan had bought that red-coloured Hyundai-i20, the most-beloved non-living object in the world to him. He orbed around the car after keeping the luggage into the dickey. He noticed a dent with couple of scratches on the right side back door, felt upset and caressed that portion.

"What happened?" Shristi asked, getting into the car.

"Nothing, just wondered to see my car in the same condition, how I left it," Adhyayan smirked.

"Why not, after all it was in Shristi's safe-hands," she said, pulling her top gently. Her innocence made Adhyayan smile.

Adhyayan had learnt from his experience, not to point out any girl's fault, especially when she is your wife or girlfriend. Few years back Shristi had driven the car over a speed-breaker, comparatively much higher in velocity than the convincing speed to cross a hump, being inattentive to look at the newly opened restaurant. The car floated in the air for a few seconds before banging on the street. Adhyayan admonished her to concentrate on the road as it damaged the car a bit. Adhyayan had expected a 'sorry' and engrossment on driving from her. However, Shristi hollered back on Adhyayan for caring for the car more than her; she could have got hurt too. She had been driving over the speed bump in the same manner until the day she came to drop Adhyayan at the airport, for his trip to USA.

"Adi, I know, you have come back for that Uday. But it's my humble request and advise as your wife that, please don't put your career in another risk," Shristi warned, moving her index finger with her head in a rhythm.

"Hmm, I will try. Put the seat belt on," Adhyayan avoided the talk and cut it short, putting the engine on ignition.

"In India, it's enough that the driver wears a seat belt; this is not US," Shristi snapped back, as she was aware what did Adhyayan's 'try' mean.

"It's not about India or US; it's about your safety. By the way, do you know what happened? " he asked.

"No, I don't know much. Raja just said that the police have arrested Uday, while he called me for your number, and it's something related to 'Schoolyard,'" she replied fastening the seat belt.

"What the fuck! That's a decent and harmless website. Why the hell would the police arrest Uday for that," Adhyayan yelled.

"Adi, mind your language and stop shouting at me. What's my fault here?" Shristi shouted, spreading her palm outwards.

"I am not shouting at you, baby. I am just getting irritated," he clarified driving.

"Then, why did you go to US leaving 'Schoolyard'?" she asked. Adhyayan attempted to answer, but Shristi interrupted, "Adi, please don't give me the shit, that it's a life-time opportunity and all that bullshit. You already got that opportunity twice before this and refused." Adhyayan shut his mouth up for a few seconds, as the initial part of his answer was going to be exactly the same.

"I left that group because, it was against my morality. I didn't like their insensitiveness to the society, but that can't be the reason of any arrest," he explained the rest.

They became silent, and their car started talking to the air after joining the highway. Though Adhyayan's eyes were on the road, he sought for the answers of the various meandering questions in his mind. Shristi's eloquent eyes looked through the car's window. Adhyayan's stupendous aloofness hadn't left many words for Shristi even after the ten months of isolation, and it made Shristi's eyes moist and vision blur.

"By the way, how did you know my flight schedule?" Adhyayan broke the silence.

"From your Gmail that you used to book the flight,"

"You are a smart girl," he appreciated.

"I am not left with any other option as my husband is a nut," she replied, looking through the window. Anger was vivid on her face.

"Let's go to some restaurant for dinner, any new in the town?" Adhyayan tried to change Shristi's mood. She didn't respond. The car took the road towards their residence.

Every success is followed by a failure

Their car passed by 'Krishna Boy's High School' on the way to their home from the airport. Adhyayan smiled musing over that day when Uday and he had arrived at that school's principal's room with their first business proposal.

"May we come in Sir?" Uday asked for permission, partly opening the door.

A plump, bald, dark, and aged man was busy reading a newspaper in the room. He turned his face from the newspaper and stared at them shortly, peeping over his thick specs and concentrated back in reading. They waited at the door for his response. After a couple of minutes, he ordered in a husky voice, "Come in," folding the newspaper assiduously, as if that was the only newspaper on earth.

"Please," he gestured them to sit on the chairs that were placed on the other side of his huge wooden table. They occupied two out of the four chairs. A giant bookshelf, computer, piled-up files, a globe, an electric coffee maker with few cups and a tray, a water-filter, a small centre-table surrounded by three small sofas – everything in that huge air-conditioned room was perfectly placed, as if someone had decorated it very passionately for an exhibition.

"Yes, you have thirty minutes. Today is Saturday, so half-day," he said, aligning his slightly tilted reddish-black, wooden nameplate perfectly on the table; 'Principal: R. V. Gowda'– it read.

"Sir, we are here with a proposal...," Uday started and stopped immediately after Mr. Gowda interrupted him.

"Look young men; uniform, textbooks, notebook, pen, pencil etc are already covered by different vendors. And we don't encourage private tuitions. Do you have anything other than these to sell?" Mr. Gowda asked, nodding on each item.

Mr. Gowda's statement incinerated Uday's hope in a blink. Uday had been exploring on business-proposals for the last few days, riffling through several sites and blogs on the internet and had also prepared few pages of presentation as well. He had rehearsed in front of the mirror for hours for that meeting, called Adhyayan several times at midnight in excitement on finding tricks to handle counter questions on a business meeting, and bribed Mr. Gowda's assistant to fix that appointment. Though, Adhyayan's sick leave was quite natural, Uday's time-off in the notice period was troublesome. However, post-tormented by the reality, he felt pity on those pages and its author. He enveloped them back into that red-file that he had been carrying chivalrously so far.

"Sir, we are not salesmen. We would like to discuss regarding our website on the schools of Bangalore," Adhyayan pioneered, realizing Uday's baffled state of mind, reading his numb face.

"Ha ha, but to me it's the same! You are here to get some money out of me, selling your product; they too do the same; only the product is different," Mr. Gowda misguided, grinning.

"You don't have to pay a single penny," Uday snapped back in frustration. Adhyayan tapped Uday on his hand, gesturing to control his emotions under the table.

"Hmmm! We have our own official website. Why should we go for yours? And what is your profit in that?" Mr. Gowda asked, playing with a pen on the table.

"Sir, the official websites always talk about a particular organization, particularly the good aspects only and mostly those are non-interactive. Our site will provide the complete picture of all schools of Bangalore comparatively, and it will provide a platform to the parents, teachers, and students to discuss studies online, sitting in the comfort of their respective homes." Adhyayan explained, hoping to impress the principal. However, he had never imagined Mr. Gowda had so much of concerns on their excellent and free service.

Mr. Gowda responded, "I am dead against these on-line communications and all this stuff. Every month, we arrange a teacher-parents meeting to discuss on students' well-being, and I believe that is the best way, the human interaction in person and we teach the same to our students. But, your site will make teachers and parents distant." He paused for a moment, reading the disbelief in their faces and continued, "Let me explain to you young men through an example. In our childhood, in rainy days we used to find excuses to go out and enjoy raindrops falling on our body. We use to make paper-boats and sail them on those puddles in front of our home. Huh! But now, my grandchildren take pictures of the rain and load them on Facebook. Then they will wait for hours to count, how many likes, and comments on it, bullshit! Pardon my language, but that's a fact. Do you think that's social network? Two neighbours, sharing a common wall, come to know about each other's whereabouts by Facebook updates; it's an anti-social network. This is American culture – individualism, separation."

"Correct, but on the other hand it provides an option to communicate with those that you can't meet in person. Everything in the world has a good and a bad side to it; it depends on the user. Moreover, most of the parents of your students are IT professionals and they don't have much time out of their jobs. Do you think that one meeting per month can cover all their concerns and requirements?" Adhyayan riposted.

"Please don't teach me. Forty-five years, I believe it's more than your age, I am in this industry. Your thirty minutes are over. You may leave now," Mr. Gowda disdained, frown faced.

Uday got up from the chair and approached the door in hurried steps, grabbing his red-file. Adhyayan followed him.

"How many schools could you fool into this trap of yours till now?" Mr. Gowda asked from behind.

"Ten Sir," Adhyayan retorted.

"Who are they?" Mr. Gowda quizzed wryly.

"That's our business's secret. Sorry, but we can't reveal until you are a part of it," Adhyayan replied. Uday glanced at him through the corner of his eyes, wondering.

"Where the fuck you got those ten schools from?" Uday asked, as soon as they came out of the room, visibly irritated.

"Just to give him some eerie feelings... As per my intuition, he will call us back. Otherwise, he wouldn't have asked that question," Adhyayan commented casually, walking towards the parking.

"I don't think so. He asked that question to insult us that's all,"

"He is a hypocrite who always tries to prove himself an odd-man-out in a gathering. In a young group, he tries to show his fondness to the old thing and shows off his ultra modern life-style to the aged people," Adhyayan explained.

"And how the hell did you know all this?" Uday asked frustratingly, being annoyed by Adhyayan's psychiatrically behaviour.

"Last night, when you informed me that we were going to meet the principal of 'Krishna Boy's High School,' I checked his Facebook timeline thoroughly."

"What the fuck! He has a Facebook account?" Uday shouted, shocked.

"Yes, he is at level 90 in Candy-crush."

*****

Uday panicked, as he stood on the auditorium-dais in front of those gazing pair of eyes that were noticing his each movement. He looked for Adhyayan nervously, but could not find him. He closed his eyes, bending his head down to turn his reckless and capricious heartbeats in rhythm. Few of his childhood's memories flashed in his mind, engraving his mental-wounds, which bled freshly, as it usually happens with him when he closes his eyes.

He looked up with moist eyes, walked a little closer to the loudspeaker and said, "We would like to convey our gratitude to all the respectable faculties and parents present here. It's a great honour to us that you managed some hours from your extremely busy schedule to listen to us. In my childhood, I had longed to perform some poetry reciting or story telling like my lucky cousins used to do in all family gatherings. However, I was treated as an intruder. Either my relatives humiliated my mother or lambasted me, on my participation attempts. Today, your spontaneous presence helps me wipe out all that. And I am feeling immense pleasure having such a big family," he paused for a few moments, wiped his moist eyes and continued after taking a long breathe, "I am Uday, and he is my friend Adhyayan. Both of us work in an IT organization." Uday pointed to Adhyayan.

Adhyayan had been standing near the projector since Uday started his speech, shocked. On his introduction, the entire audience turned their face towards him, and he waved his hand softly, grinning like a laggard.

"We are here to invite you to be a part of India's first interactive website for schools. Adhyayan, the first slide please," Uday requested. Adhyayan played the slide show on which they had worked on the complete day last Sunday, at Adhyayan's flat. They had built some tentative pictorial representations of their website as Shristi had suggested. According to Shristi, pictures are much more expressive, attractive, and easy to understand than words. Hence, they discarded their well-known boring official style of bullet-points and paragraphs.

Uday continued once the first slide glowed on the screen, "This site will demolish all the obstacles of communication between teachers and parents."

Uday took a little pause and threw a question to audience, "Tell me, how many of us have the time to visit the school daily?"

"None of us, but it's equally important as our other commitments," Uday continued answering his own question on seeing the audience silent. "This site will give a common platform to both teachers and parents to share their views on a day-to-day basis. In our site, each student will have a page like this…." Uday explained every minute detail about the website; where the student's picture will be posted, where all the subjects will be listed, how on clicking any subjects, the timetable, and a unit test schedule will pop-up for that particular subject and many more features.

As much as Uday had been unfolding each picture, the audience had slumped into those.

'CRS Convent High School', one of the famous schools in Bangalore, was listed in the last few to be approached, while their website could build a reputation. However, they got an opportunity to visit that school in second place. They weren't trespassers this time; rather they managed a reference, Thirumalai Chinnasami, an influential teacher of 'CRS Convent High School' and Adhyayan's neighbour. Thirumalai's wife and Shristi had an acquaintanceship, built eventually through 'neighbouring techniques' like salt, sugar, tea, milk etc exchange. Shristi suggested Adhyayan to have a discussion with Thirumalai, while she heard about that botched meeting with Mr. Gowda. A meeting was scheduled on Monday during the lunch break at the school auditorium. As Adhyayan and Uday were not prepared yet, for big schools as 'CRS Convent High School'. They had to put together an immense effort to prepare that presentation.

As soon as Uday reached the last page of their presentation titled 'Questions' few teachers and parents darted their queries as Uday and Adhyayan were expecting.

"This will be a pain for us. After class we have to spend time on replying to parents' enquiries," one of the faculty members replied, as soon as Adhyayan handed over the mouthpiece.

"Agreed Sir, initially, it will demand little extra level of efforts. But since parents will start taking part in their kids study, indirectly it will reduce the teachers' effort effectively. Sir, please think, while you are admitting that there is a possibility of huge parents' enquiries, then this service becomes mandatory and it's the school's responsibility to fulfil that. Are you with me Sir?" Uday retorted.

Adhyayan ran down to a father, who stood up to collect the next question, "Don't you think, this will create pressure on the students?"

"No, Sir, in fact we would be able to understand them more intimately. There won't be anything for them to hide from you and, as a result, all kind of unpleasant surprises can be avoided," Adhyayan answered, getting back the loudspeaker.

"And how much do we have to pay for this service?" one woman in the audience asked.

"Nothing as of now, it's a free service for the first six months after the launch. Thereafter, a parent has to pay only thousand rupees per year, not even hundred rupees per month. Is it fine ma'am?" Uday replied. She nodded, smiling in satisfaction.

"What will be the name of your site? I haven't seen any name in those slides," the principal asked.

Uday and Adhyayan exchanged glances seeking help. They had thought over each micro detailing in spite of that time crunch, but missed that simple but important part. The unnerving thought of spoiling all their hard work for that stupid mistake, made Uday frown tensed. His obsessed mind had traumatized responsively on any slight threat of his dream.

"Sir, we decided to keep this website anonymous. We would like to give you, 'CRS Convent High School' the honour to name it. Could you please suggest a good name Sir?" Adhyayan defended the situation, vigorously.

The audience broke into twittering, proposing names as per their point of views. Adhyayan opened a notepad and jotted down all the names that were being proposed. Finally, the website got a name, 'The Schoolyard' after few rounds of discussion and debate.

"Can we have a round of applauds for 'The Schoolyard'?" Uday pricked the audience. The sound of the audience's applause echoed in the auditorium, ricocheting from each nook and corner. Uday felt as if some soft hand petting the wounds of his puerility life; a chilled and bloodcurdling wave blew through his nerves. He couldn't help controlling the oozed out droplets of water to glide through from his eyes.

They started for their office, quenched, securing a conformation mail from 'CRS Convent High School' to join them.

"Good job Uday," Adhyayan appreciated, while driving back to the office.

"You are my man buddy. It wouldn't have been possible without your help," Uday responded, patting Adhyayan's shoulder.

"By the way, what was the shit you started your speech with?" Adhyayan enquired, stopping the car on a signal.

"Bullshit! Just read that trick in a blog to engage the listeners," Uday said followed by a loud laugh and a couple of claps. "How magically it works, right?" he continued. Adhyayan nodded expressing his agreement. Adhyayan started the car on the signal turning green, humming the song – *'Tum itna jo muskura rahe ho, kya gam hai jisko chhupa rahe ho.'* (*What are you trying to hide by your smile?*) Uday switched the music system on loudly, complaining about Adhyayan's choice of song and voice.

*****

The days that followed, they had gone through a squeezed timetable. They utilized the time, optimally out of their office-schedule. All infrastructure related hustles they had covered during the daytime for the obvious reasons of dependency on others and busied themselves at night to write the artefacts. Uday had economic conservation to pursue his dream project, but Adhyayan had to stake Shristi's and his hard-earned money, which was preserved for their flat to rent an office, buy computers, hire techies, register 'The Schoolyard' officially as a company, get a Domain-Name and Web-Host. As the domain name, 'Schoolyard.com' had already been sold to an

American website; they had to opt for a different domain name, 'Scho0lyard.com,' apparently lookalike.

Mostly college students attended the interview responding to their advertisement on Bangalore's local newspapers, and they selected six college students, who had exuberance, analytical and technical skills, craving for money, but experience. Uday summoned Rajasekaran driven by his indulgent to lead that young brigade.

Rajasekaran's groomed appearance stupefied Adhyayan and Uday, when he arrived at that residential flat that they had rented as an office.

"What's wrong?" Rajasekaran asked, louring as he noticed their open-mouthed and popeyed faces. His sandal marked forehead was clean; moustache was neatly shaved and his hair was trimmed short at the sides and back, leaving the front and middle spiked long. He looked like a dude in a slim fit linen shirt and torn jeans. The fragrance of his perfume swept over the new paint's smell on the walls.

"Nothing wrong, but suddenly what happened to you? I saw you at office last Friday," Uday wondered.

That was the consequence of consorting with Sneha, but Rajasekaran replied suppressing the truth, "Just for a change," as he was not yet affirmed about Sneha's feelings – was that love, friendship, just time-pass or benignity. They had been hanging around together after office since last week. On that Saturday, she took him to an expensive salon and instructed the hairdresser throughout. She made Rajasekaran spend his money on modern attires of her choice. They watched an English movie after a long argument on proving the superiority of each other's maternal languages; Bengali and Tamil, followed by lunch at a Non-vegetarian restaurant, where Rajasekaran merely found something for vegetarians like him. He agreed on all her wishes to buy her a promise of quitting all addicting habits. She promised to quit drinking; however smoking was arduous for her to leave instantly.

"Ok, coming to the main point. We need your help," Adhyayan said and placed all the documents they prepared on 'Schoolyard' in front of Rajasekaran.

He leafed through the pages randomly and said excitedly, "Could you allow me to design it in my way?"

"Yes," Adhyayan and Uday replied in unison, looking at Rajasekaran for his next reaction.

"It's an awesome idea! But I can't do it all alone," he abandoned after an impermanent excitement.

"Yes of course, we have hired six college students. They don't have any real-time hands on experience, but they are smart," Uday assured, lighting a cigarette and continued placing the lighter on the table, "One issue... they will be working starting from evening to night. Is that ok for you?"

"That's depending on you. If you allow me to leave office early," Rajasekaran replied, smiling.

"I have resigned; some new guy will join as your lead," Uday shrugged, emitting a chest full of smoke.

Rajasekaran hadn't come out of that shock completely when Adhyayan asked, "Would you like to be Schoolyard's business partner or employee?"

"Business Partner, obviously," he answered, giggling.

"In that case for the first one year, you have to work without any profits or returns," Adhyayan said and Rajasekaran's denture vanished back inside his mouth.

"No pain, no gain!" Uday added.

"Deal," Rajasekaran agreed and placed his hand firmly on the table over the document; Uday and Adhyayan followed him.

Pursuit of desire

The warm air coupled with the glittering yellow ray from the partially nibbled sun of twilight that was present, just a moment ago, was replaced by a huffing chilled wind that rose, tugging a crawling, dark-gray, gigantic cloud behind and concealed the sky entirely. The curtains at the next building's window, the shrivelled clothes on the roofs and tree leaves undulated untidily, as if they were on a protest for freedom. In a couple of minutes, it began pouring with pitter-patter all over. Two little girls started dancing in the rain on the rooftop. Crazy wind goaded raindrops fell on Shristi's face. However, she had been basking in those little ones' dances indifferently, smiling since they had started. The wind turned wilder; more rainwater began dashing through the balcony that drenched Shristi. Slowly, as the smile on her face lingered, she sobbed.

She had not noticed when Adhyayan had reached home and stood behind her, brooded in her loneliness. It was a Sunday morning, so Shristi woke up late and since then she had been waiting for Adhyayan to come back home. He cuddled her by her waist from behind and kissed her on her neck.

"Everything is set now. We have arranged the power-backup as well, the last thing that was left. From next Monday, our work will start and after three months we are targeting to launch India's first interactive website for schools, Schoolyard. I am excited baby," Adhyayan said, embracing Shristi tightly. A woman came up to the roof and toted those little girls on her lap, out of the roof.

"Congrats!" She felicitated, spraining her face back, looking at Adhyayan. Her moist, awfully hurt eyes turned Adhyayan's excitement in agitation. He caressed her face by his palms assiduously and whispered, "What's wrong baby?" A belligerent lightening vanished in the dark cloud, reaching the horizon originating from the middle of the sky, followed by a cracking sound.

"Adi, Where am I in your life?" she asked, removing the wet hair that was falling on her face.

"Did I hurt you by any means Shristi? Please tell me precisely. I was entirely occupied by Schoolyard's stuff... so..." He asked embracing her tightly. Rainfall had been playing the tag-game boisterously with the haphazard wind and splashed on them.

"That money was for your flat and my baby Adi. I don't care about your damn flat, but you made that dependency on taking a baby," she wept, contorted. Adhyayan stood speechlessly like a corpse; he had no words to console Shristi. He had never realized when Uday's dream had become his and destroyed Shristi's.

"I'm extremely sorry baby. I didn't realize that in the excitement. But don't worry; we will get double that money back, soon. Just see, after our website launches. We will fulfil all our wishes and dreams," Adhyayan tried to bring solace.

"Adi, it's not about money; it's about my importance in your life. You didn't even feel the urge consult with me once, and that is hurting me," she retorted, relinquishing herself from his arms, crying. Adhyayan grimaced repenting on his callousness. The rain had become heavier gradually as time passed. She attempted to leave the balcony, steeping inside the room. He pulled her clasping her wet waist and whispered kissing her ears, "Let's have a baby!"

"Just because I cried, right? I don't want to Adi, until you don't feel it," Shristi muttered, closing her eyes quivering at his touch.

"I feel it; just the feeling fainted a bit because of this work pressure," he stated in a low apologetic tone. He nibbled her lips in his mouth. Shristi kissed him back.

"Do you have the plan for any public show on the balcony?" Shristi asked smiling. Adi lifted her up in his arms and came inside the room laughing. He laid her on the bed, neglecting her conscious protest on getting the bed wet. He removed her T-shirt and bra, and started cuddling her.

"Did you research anything on Google about it?" he asked curiously kissing her breast.

"On what?" she asked pushing him away in shock.

"No, I mean, I heard that the baby's structure, intelligence, looks, and all other attributes can be controlled by the mating procedure... Am I wrong?" he fumbled to explain. Shristi burst into huge laughter.

"Bullshit! Just forget everything in this world and pour your heart out on me," she responded seductively tugging him to fall on her, and whispered, "That's it. Your baby will be exactly how you want!"

*****

When Uday, Adhyayan, and Rajasekaran reached Schoolyard's office in the evening, their selected six college students were waiting outside the flat. Their unconventional attire, bags on their shoulder, unruly attitude, and contemplation on their mobile reminded Adhyayan of his puerility's tuition classes.

"We should have arranged for a security guard. It's embarrassing," Uday whispered, opening the door and inviting all inside. It was a usual residential flat consisting of two bedrooms, one hall, two bathrooms and one kitchen. They made the comparatively bigger bedroom, their meeting-room for discussions on business related strategies and the other one for technical training and discussions. The hall was dedicated as the primary working floor, furnished by several small tables, chairs, and computers. They had arranged a micro oven, a refrigerator, and a gas stove along with a handful of utensils for the kitchen.

"Uday, don't you think they are too young to work? Look at them; they are just college students, kids. I think we should take their parents' permission first," Adhyayan asked in a low voice, emotionally.

"I checked their date of birth; they are all eighteen plus and are allowed to work in India, legally. They are much better here than working in some restaurant or some other bullshit. They will learn a hell lot of technical stuff, which will be helpful for their future," Uday tried to convince Adhyayan practically.

"Welcome to 'The Schoolyard' family," Uday greeted loudly, while all of them settled down.

"Thank you, sir," few of them replied in chorus.

"No sir and all, call me Uday. He is Adhyayan, and his name is Rajasekaran. Raja is your tech-lead, and will guide you in all technical issues. In his absence, you can reach out to Adhyayan or me. On weekdays, we will meet here in the evening for the obvious reason of your colleges and our office and on weekends at anytime, if we really need to work. We won't follow any fucking dress code or working hours. The security guard will get you the key at any time you need. But the deliverable should be completed on time. Are you with me?" Uday proclaimed, raising his hand.

"Yes Uday," all of them shouted, laughing.

"Cool! Now look at these papers carefully. They are quite self-explanatory, right? Go through them and bring them filled up by tomorrow. Just one rule we will all have to obey, any 'Schoolyard' related communication shouldn't be done through your personal mails or devices. We have to use only our official mailbox and computer for the same. All your system credentials are mentioned in one of these papers," Uday paused for a moment, while Adhyayan distributed those papers among them.

"Now, the most-interesting part guys is the salary that we are here for, 7000 bucks per month, is it fine?" Uday asked, smiling mischievously.

"Yes," some of them responded with high-five and some nodded to convey the same.

"If we do well, we will get more. Are you with me?" Uday spurred loudly.

"Yes, Uday," they shouted in spontaneously.

"Cool! You can leave for the day."

Adhyayan started for home early concerned about Shristi. He had seen Shristi to be fatigued and emotionally tensed, even after she had been notified about his late arriving at home. However, Uday and Rajasekaran spent almost the entire night discussing on the technical designs and approaches that day.

The next three consecutive months passed in rigours of a tight work schedule, especially for Uday. In the morning, Adhyayan had been picking him up from his place to visit some schools before reaching office and in the night, he had to work with Rajasekaran on technical stuff. Perhaps, his passion for accomplishing his dream and obtaining success rendered an internal power that refrained him from being exhausted. They had succeeded to enlist five more schools under Schoolyard, as a win over 'CRS Convent High School' helped them to convince other schools effortlessly.

That was the last Sunday before 'Schoolyard' was going to be live on the internet. Rajasekaran had been demonstrating the different aspects of 'Schoolyard' to Adhyayan and Uday.

"Raja, you are a fucking genius man. I knew it; you are 'the man,'" Uday appreciated in his style, lighting a cigarette.

"The design is yours Uday; I just implemented it," Rajasekaran stated generously and after a pause he asked, "Aren't you happy with the design?" noticing Adhyayan, introspectively gazing at the screen.

"No, it's absolutely fine, just curious about this button, 'Take a tour,'" Adhyayan said pointing at the screen.

"This is my master stroke, out of Uday's design. We can't go to each and every parent or teacher to show how this site works right?" Rajasekaran started explaining. Uday leaned his frowned face back on the screen, abruptly abandoning his relaxed and sit back posture. Adhyayan nodded.

"Hence, in that case, this button will help them understand each nook and corner of this website with voice dictation. They just have to click this button, sit back, and watch," he said clicking the button.

A blonde girl in a black skirt, white formals, and high pencil-heels appeared on the screen and introduced herself as the teacher of 'Schoolyard.' She described all the graphical user interfaces and their functionality, slightly seductively and in an American accent. That eloquent presentation could satiate an unaccustomed person of a computer to use 'Schoolyard' naturally.

Uday and Adhyayan watched that presentation, popeyed till the schoolyard's self-proclaimed teacher said, 'Bye' and turned towards Rajasekaran, dazed. Rajasekaran waved his eyebrow, expecting an enormous appreciation from them. However, their reactions were not likewise.

"Why the fuck does she have a tattoo on her leg? Why the hell the buttons of her shirt are open? Why does she talk so erotically?" Adhyayan and Uday retorted one by one.

"Chumma!" Rajasekaran murmured like a dawdler, nervously.

Uday and Adhyayan were obdurate to make that 'Take a tour' functionality dormant, until Rajasekaran corrects the pointed out concerns. According to Uday, that animated woman should wear a sari as any Indian lady-teacher does. However, Adhyayan convinced him to agree on skirt and shirt noticing Rajasekaran's contorted face on Uday's decision, saying sari would be more exposing. After a long debate, Uday and Adhyayan agreed to have a tattoo as well on Rajasekaran's repetitive request, but not those open-buttons.

*****

Finally, 'Schoolyard' launched with six schools. Through rollercoaster rides of different technical issues, it ran for the next three months. That trio's technical proficiency never allowed any such consequence to be an obstacle on the way of their dream. But the survival of 'Schoolyard' till the demise of the free-subscription period was the biggest challenge for them, another three months. In the past six months, Uday and Adhyayan had already spent all their lay asides.

It was the fourth time that Adhyayan had been riffling through all three of his bank accounts, since he reached Schoolyard's office that evening, expecting a magical calculation to pop up some money. Uday had quit his job almost six months ago; he was surviving somehow on a handful of his leftover savings. He had been staying at the office to avert the cost of a separate rental residence. Rajasekaran had just started his professional life, and merely had some saving. The thought of Schoolyard's succumbing shattered Adhyayan. He rushed to the hall for Uday.

"Guys, you have been doing a phenomenal job. All the issues reported by our customers have been resolved within twenty-four hours, and they are triumphal with our service. I have been receiving lots of appreciation mails from parents and teachers alike. Let's have a round of applauds for ourselves," Uday goaded the team-Schoolyard to cheer. Everyone present at that floor clapped spontaneously, including that newly constituted security-guy, Chandra. Certainly he had no clue regarding the reason of applauding, but he realized those people who had given him a job are blissful. His ingenuousness, the proud and beaming faces of Uday and the others, pulled Adhyayan's feet back. He stood there for few minutes confoundedly.

"Other than those appreciation mails, I got an interesting mail also from a worried father, who wants to hide all the communication between him and the teachers from his smart son. Hence, our next work is to tune that security level. I have already shared the design to Raja; he will guide you through the coding. And...," Uday continued.

Adhyayan came back to his chair leaving the hall. He thought of calling Shristi if she can help them out of that financial crisis somehow for another three months. He called her, but hung up within few seconds in remorse. He thought of calling his parents or few of his schools friends, but that didn't appear right to him. He threw his arms on the table before him and hid his face.

"What the fuck? We are working our arse off, and you are sleeping here," Uday taunted entering the room. Adhyayan reared slowly from the table and looked at Uday with blank and emotionless eyes.

"What is fucking wrong with you, bitten by some Zombie?" Uday mocked cackling.

"Not feeling well. I am leaving man."

Adhyayan left abruptly before Uday could read his psyche. In the past few occasions, he noticed Uday being traumatised whenever any jeopardy sprang up for 'Schoolyard'. He knew that he had to speak up about it one or the other day to Uday, but not before, he had been defeated by the circumstances, though he had no clue where to get the money.

A sluggish depression grasped Adhyayan. He couldn't sleep that night. The next day, in the evening they all gathered again at Schoolyard's office.

"Guys, we have to expand Schoolyard," Uday said with an air of satisfaction, turning his laptop's screen towards Adhyayan and Rajasekaran. The screen showed an acceptation mail from 'Joseph Collegiate High School', one of the biggest and prestigious schools of Bangalore. Rajasekaran upraised his palm excitedly for a high-five and hit Uday's.

"What has happened to you? Aren't you happy?" Uday asked, observing Adhyayan's dimmed reaction.

"Nothing, I am happy. By the way, what do you mean by expanding then? It's expanding right," Adhyayan vacuously asked.

"I meant; we need to increase our team strength and infrastructure to handle this business expansion. This flat and this small team are not enough."

Adhyayan felt an impulse to yell that they were broke. He stifled his frustration but the truth. "Uday, we don't have money to run this show for another three months, charitably. Just forget about more investment and all. We need to make this a paid service, right away," Adhyayan informed calmly, trying hard to conceal the rigours.

"We shouldn't break our commitment. Somehow we have to continue our free service," Uday blabbered, whispering.

A silence embraced the room momentarily until Rajasekaran's cell phone rang. He pulled the phone out of his pocket hesitatingly and peeped at the screen under the table. A message had arrived from Sneha – 'Hey *Sambar* J What's up?' A smile waved on Rajasekaran's face instinctively as he remembered Sneha's philosophy of naming someone. He wore a gloomy face instantly after lifting up his eyes from his mobile. He looked at Adhyayan and Uday, worriedly.

"Adi, tell... me one Bengali sweet's name?" He asked awkwardly. Adhyayan and Uday looked at him, smouldering without any response as if he had stolen all their money and was caught red-handed.

"*Misti doi, (Sweet yogurt)*" Adhyayan replied after a moment, staring.

'In a serious meeting... What about you *misti doi*? J' – He replied back not tampering the mask of his serious expression.

"We have only one week left for month end, and we have to pay the salary, rent of this flat, electric bill and blah-blah... Otherwise, we have to stop Schoolyard here," Adhyayan blabbered monotonously.

"I know Adi! I got it clearly," Uday hollered, banging on the table loudly. What happened was exactly what Adhyayan was scared of. He regretted. The pain of being obliged to practise concealment towards Uday was little inferior to the pain of having made him distressed. The room plunged in silence.

Sneha's message buzzed again, 'Hmm... smrt ass! J Let's go fr misti doi... hav u evr had?'

'Tomorrow?' – Rajasekaran texted back as it was impracticable for him to abscond from that room until they were not arriving at a decisive point of a solution.

'Nooooo... rt nw... r u cmin or ntL?' Sneha messaged back in less than a second.

"We should try for some sponsors and advertisements from the local, but big shops for school-stuff," Rajasekaran suggested, hoping to conclude that discussion.

"Yes, that's a good idea," Uday beguiled, as if a chain-smoker had found a half-burnt cigarette from the trash in a crisis, though Adhyayan was optimistic. They planned to visit all the shops of their consequent localities in the next few days.

Relations absorb and ooze pain

As Sneha had asked him through the phone texted messages, Rajasekaran reached K.C Das, the authentic Bengali sweet shop near M.G road. After ten odd minutes, she arrived there in her usual funky attire. She waved at Rajasekaran and went inside the shop; he followed her.

"*Kaku, duto eksho gram kore doi dao na,*" (Uncle, give hundred grams of curd in two plates.) Sneha requested an aged waiter, who was busy in cleaning the nearby table after occupying a corner table for them.

"*Arr kichhu? Gorom kochuri ache maa, debo?*" (Anything else? Hot *Kachori* is there dear; should I bring?) that aged person asked, smiling affectionately.

"*Na kaku, onno ek din khabo,*" (No uncle, some other day) Sneha replied with a sweet smile. Rajasekaran had no hint about that conversation, but he wore a droning grinning-face like a bride at her in-laws' place during the reception.

"Can I ask you something?" Rajasekaran asked on the waiter's divergence. Sneha nodded inclining her face on the table attentively.

"Why are you like this?"

"What do you mean? ...like what?" She asked back, though she guessed his connotation, she wanted to confirm.

"I mean... like how you are, how you carry yourself, your dressing, lifestyle, carefree attitude towards life," he carefully and slowly manifested, averting hurting her by any means, "and tattoos," he added after a pause. In the meanwhile 'the *misti doi*' was served on their table in clay-pots. Sneha thanked the waiter smiling formally.

"Do you have any problem with that?" she slurred, basking in a mouthful of sweet-yogurt. A droplet fell on her chin under her lower lips.

"Nope... I like it, just curious about a friend, who thinks I am close..." he said cajolingly. Sneha beamed her eyes followed by a suppressed hint of a smile. "Your parents don't have any objection? After all you are from an Indian family," he continued curiously.

"Objection?" She laughed ironically and continued post a solicitous interruption, "I am dying for their objections since I started sensing their aloofness for me. I tried hard to seek their attention. My outstanding results in class and my singing, all failed. Then I started showing them my spoilt, carefree life and ended up, how I am today. Still they couldn't find anything odd about me but others like you. I had barely seen my parents at home. Seema *masi*, their appointed nanny, had taken care of me. She was pitiable materialistically, but richer than my parents by heart," she stopped, sighing in depression. She tried hard to smile with moist eyes and quivering lips.

"But that day when your mother called, she sounded concerned... Worried. It might be your wrong perception also, nah?" he said after a protracted hush to console her.

"That's for their so called high society," she retorted, gesturing quotes. "For the last couple of weeks that call has started coming for convincing me to get married to one of their rich-client's son. So, she just wanted to check whether I am alive, maybe not raped, or murdered. Mr. Debraj Bose, my father, the jewellery king, and Mrs. Debjani Bose, my mother, a high profile interior designer of Kolkata, doesn't have time for me. The wrong perception was that like others, I too considered myself, the luckiest daughter, born with a silver spoon," she snivelled in a single breath and stopped. Drops of tears glided through her pink cheeks, liquefying the black mascara from her eyes.

Rajasekaran had a glance over the shop a bit bewildered, to confirm no one was observing them. The shop was quite empty as it was near their closing time. All the workers were busy in preserving the sweets and scavenging the shop. He never had been in that circumstance before. He left his chair and occupied the empty one by her at another side of the table.

"Snega, please don't cry," he whispered, inclining his face near to her.

"When I had grown up, I started finding friends around me and made few as well. But slowly I realized, they had other priorities or notions; no one cared for me," she burst out sobbing.

"I do Snega and will do it life long," he solaced, wiping her tears. She nodded her consent. To her surprise, he rubbed his thumb on her chin to clean the yogurt and said, "*Misti Doi.*"

"*Tui ki amae bhalobashis Sambar?*" she asked smiling naughtily. He gestured curiously to translate in English, but Sneha laughed at him.

As tit for tat he replied, "*Enakku unnoda moli puriyalai. Anal nan unnai kadhalikeren misti doi.*" She burst into a huge heartfelt laughter.

*****

Adhyayan lit a cigarette, standing at the balcony. It started the dawn after another of his sleep-deprived nights. A freezing wind scurried on his tired eyes, extorting tears. Rajasekaran's plan didn't work. They approached almost all the school stationary retailers of Bangalore. Some of them repudiated, as they were unaccustomed with the concept of online advertising and its benefits in their business, where others were satiated by the economic promotion activities through local cable-channels. What is next? The question had been haunting him all the time.

"Good morning darling," Shristi hugged him from the back.

Adhyayan shockingly looked back, regressing from an absentminded state about surroundings, and replied, "Morning." He pulled her in front and kissed her on the forehead.

"I have good news for you. Any guesses?" she said kissing back his lips.

"Got any award or bonus?" he asked.

"Mr. Adhyayan Roy, can you think about anything other than career or money?" she mocked tapping his nose softly. "I am pregnant," she said, hiding her face on his chest embracing him tightly.

"Really!" he wondered and hugged her back tightly.

"What are you expecting, a girl, or boy? I need a girl. Even your mother had said long back that she wished to have a granddaughter. I have decided a name also for our daughter, Adarshi. How is it? See, it has both of our...," Shristi stopped beguiled breathlessly in a motherhood fantasy and stopped observing Adhyayan's insularism after a while.

"Are you listening?" she asked not getting any response even after she had muted.

"Hmm, yes... yes I am listening. Do we have money saved somewhere?" he asked fumbling.

"Yes, I have some two lakhs in LIC. Why, are you worried about the cost of delivery, medicine and all?" she enquired curiously.

"No, we still have a few months for that. I need that money within this week to rescue Schoolyard. Can you withdraw that amount? I will return it to you in the next four months," he requested with buoyant eyes that didn't allow Shristi to do anything other than nodding her sanction.

"Thank you, baby," he bosomed her, kissing on her lips and said, "Quickly, get ready. We have to go to the LIC office now. Let me call Uday in the meanwhile." He went inside the room.

Shristi stood there limply, shocked at Adhyayan's behaviour. How could Schoolyard get precedence over his child; was his accord with the decision of having baby an act of recompense; had he cared about her; had he ever loved her or was it his immaturity to prioritize crave over obligation? She interrogated herself. The twinge of conscience made her feel unheeded and swindled; she started crying.

Adhyayan headed to Schoolyard's office as Uday's cell phone was out of coverage and learnt about his departure for Rajasthan in the morning.

*****

"Do you have any wish to marry before my death? At least I can die in peace then," Uday's mother asked worriedly, while he had been gulping the food scrumptiously.

"*Maa*, I am exhausted of these questions. Now, please let me have my food," Uday answered back, disturbed.

"Ok. But I need an answer today," she admonished hurriedly and left the room.

Uday hit the hay soon after ceasing the deprivation of his mother's cooked food that he used to long for all the time in Bangalore. The fatigue of that elongated journey comprising of a flight, train, auto, and cart to reach his birthplace, Tripali

Badi village from Bangalore made him slumber instantly. Almost after seven long years he had returned to Tripali Badi, since he had started his professional life in Bangalore, as that village had never let Uday weaken the retentiveness of his perturbed childhood. His homecoming was just a desperate attempt to rescue Schoolyard, selling the only left off property of his father's shattered empire, a plot of land. Though he was much cognizant that his mother would get hurt and maybe could remonstrate too, but he had no alternative. Uday already had experienced her austerity, while he had jeopardized that plot to cope an educational loan for pursuing his engineering career.

His mother arrived back with the same hope of securing a pledge on his marriage and smiled finding him sleeping in a juvenile posture, snoring. She fondled his hair kissing on the forehead and left.

"Uday, I am getting old. Like all mothers, I too have a wish to see my son's wife, to play with my grandchild. Can't you fulfil your mother's pure desire?" She started again handing over the teacup in the morning.

"Hmm... do you have biscuits?" he asked to circumvent the topic.

She brought the intact biscuit packet from the kitchen, kept it on the table in front of him, and stared at him dourly. "What?" he asked simpering at her adolescent act.

"Finish the biscuit packet, but I need my answer today. On the phone, you do all the dramas to avoid me, but now you are in front me and not doing anything important. So no more lies and escape," she reprimanded, settling on the chair opposite to him.

"Maa please; I have a lot of things left to do still. I can't think about marriage and all right now."

"Listen Uday; don't try to pull the wool over my eyes, enough of your excuses. I am listening to this since the last two years," she screamed and asked softly after a solicitous pause, "Do you like any girl?" Uday nodded his incongruity, sipping his tea. "Then any boy?" she whispered, contorting her face.

"What the ...," he tugged his tongue to be slipped and continued, "No, nothing like that." She sighed slacking and smiled.

Their conversation got interrupted on Irfan's arrival. As per the discussion over the phone with Uday, he reached his home sharply at nine. Irfan, professionally a controller, started working for Uday's father while his business just embarked on and never left him, even at the coarse time while Uday's father could not pay him. Uday admired him for his trustworthiness and confronting attitude to problems. Irfan used to call Uday as Yuvraj endearingly as he was his king's son.

"*Arey* Irfan *bhai*, come in. Let me bring some tea for you," Uday's mother greeted him delightedly and approached towards the kitchen.

"*Bhabi*... without sugar. Getting old, so doctor has asked to control," Irfan requested laughing. She left consenting with him.

"So *Yuvraj*, how can I help you?" he asked adorably.

"I want to sell that plot. I don't want to go for any tight bargain; just need the money quickly, by this weekend. Any price that seems reasonable to you, I am fine with that. Can you help me get a customer?" Uday asked explaining.

"Little difficult as it's a remote village, let me see. Give me some..." before Irfan could finish his words Uday's Mother squawked entering the room, "No way! How can you do that Uday? That's your father's last memory."

"*Maa*, I need money to set up a business at Bangalore. And until this is not done, I can't promise you to marry anyone," Uday tried to mould intimidating her psychologically.

She came near to Uday and said caressing him on the head, "Business? Why do you need to do all that business and all? You are doing a job there, and I am happy with whatever you are sending to me. Have I asked you anything that you can't afford? Just send me thousand rupees per month; it's more than enough for me."

"I have quit the job and have started a business; two of my friends are helping me. If I don't get this money, I have to stop the business. Please try to understand," Uday explained softly holding her palms tightly.

"What? Why? Don't you know this business killed your father?" she screamed sobbing inconsolably. Uday regretted unfolding the truth. He just wanted to convince his mother somehow. Irfan had nothing to do, but sit there as a mute spectator.

Uday snarled loudly being impatient, "No one killed him. He escaped leaving us here to die, never thought about us. He was an escapee; a coward and ...." She slapped him before he could say anything more and left the room hurriedly, snivelling.

*****

"Come on! This is a flat, not an office," Sneha commented, while stepping inside Schoolyard's office.

"This is a temple," Rajasekaran whispered emotionally and after a pause continued, "At least for me, Uday and Adi. This is the breeding place of the first Indian interactive website for schools."

"Oh ho!"

Sneha had an urge to visit Schoolyard's office since she had heard about it from Rajasekaran and Uday's absence had widened that way for Rajasekaran. Though he had to manage Chandra somehow, but that was not difficult. She glinted over all the printouts of algorithms; date marked calendar with individual notes, do's-and-don'ts, to-do-list etc. stuck on the hall's wall and looked at him impressed.

"Done?" he asked. She nodded her approval. "Now, Let me take you to the logical tour of Schoolyard," he said excitedly booting one of the computers. He clicked on the 'take a tour' button of the website. She pulled a chair and started watching that animated video musingly, expressing a soft hint of a smile on her glossy lips.

"Guess? Who did it?" he asked impatiently before the video had ended, pulling another chair close to her.

"Oh my God, such a tuff question!" She mocked pretending innocent speciously, then voiced loudly, "You! because Adi and Uday hasn't seen me yet, stupid." He smiled delightedly on the accomplishment of his intent.

"Though, Uday provided the high-level design; I coded this entire site," he said, smiling and his shining eyes shone of great gratification and he continued, "It's my dream to code the end-to-end of a system, commercially."

"Good! By the way, how are you guys getting revenues?" she asked, gazing at the screen attentively.

Suddenly, to her surprise he caressed the rose tattooed on her neck. She closed her eyes in an internal shiver. "Don't you feel pain?" he whispered close to her ear. She nodded. He kissed that rose with trembling lips. Rajasekaran could feel the brisk gallop of his heart on the ribs. He pulled her on his lap. He inhaled a lungful of the sweet fragrance of her perfume. She kissed him on his lips unbuttoning her shirt. He pawed her all over, where she was uncovered out of her bra and jean-shorts. He kissed that artistic feather, tattooed on the left pulp of her partly divulged breasts. She grasped his hair deliriously. They crawled down from the chair on the floor snuggling in each other's arms. She lay on the floor straight; closing her eyes bestowing herself to Rajasekaran. He kissed all the tattoos on her hands, thigh, back, neck, and abdomen; played with the ring pierced through the thin skin of her pulsating navel. She pulled his face near hers and sucked his lips. She opened his shirt. They savoured the texture of each other's body, in a tight embrace.

Sneha twisted her hand back to unhook her bra, but Rajasekaran gripped her hand and whispered, "No. If we get married someday," Sneha's face glowed in admiration, eyes got moist in respect. She hugged him. They spent hours laid in each other's arms basking the satiated affection of their relationship.

"Hey, it's two. I can't go back to my PG," Sneha said shockingly, looking at Rajasekaran's watch and sat up freeing herself from his arms.

"Don't go please, stay with me tonight," he requested, wearing a puppyish expression. She smiled and lay back on him.

"I was thinking about your parents; they are cool, you know. My parents never gave me freedom like yours. They like me to be dependent on them for every small thing. They want me to seek their guidance even in chewing a chocolate, dressing, or combing, still now. I am tired," said Rajasekaran breathing deeply.

"Do you take me to be stupid? You just are consoling me; all parents do that as they care about their children," she replied dully.

"It's not care anymore. It's his insecurity, increasing day by day after his retirement," Rajasekaran agitatedly said in a louder voice. She kissed on his forehead, caressing his hair to tranquillize.

He continued, "It's a very normal family for our relatives or any outsiders, very calm, composed, decent, and gentle family. But for us, it's a jail. My father wants all of us to live his life, talk like him, walk like him, eat like him, and even think like him. He has never allowed me to wear clothes as per my wish, no sleeveless shirt, or t-shirt, jeans. Forget about me, anyway, I am a male. Think about my sisters; they are not allowed to do any make-up,"

"Oh my God!" Sneha exclaimed and threw a question in the next breath, "But you were saying, it's very calm and composed. Then how does he control you guys?"

"Emotional torture... starving... behaving abnormal... If that doesn't work, he threatens to commit suicide," he half-heartedly completed the sentence fumbling. Both of them spent few moments speechlessly. Sneha noticed stagnant droplets at the corner of Rajasekaran's eyes. She wiped his eyes and kissed on them.

"Ok then, we will exchange our parents after marriage," she said giggling to console him. He laughed.

*****

Uday lit a cigarette. That night, he gave up all his dreams. He had been nurturing them muffled cautiously in his heart for long. The merciless reality endured in front him to choke them aggressively until death. He consoled his heart cogitating; a moral human should not long for any dream's fulfilment, as eventually he had to die leaving everything behind. He had grown up listening to his mother's inconsolable sobbing every night. He had wanted to refurbish her submissive life in a relative's house, and all his efforts were for that accomplishment. He repented for hurting her. His retrospection interrupted while the cigarette burnt down to touch his finger; he shook his hand in reflex expressing the pain, "Ouch!"

Suddenly, the old, rusted door of his room opened slowly, clanging. His mother's shadow elongated on the floor stopping the beam of light, peeping through the door from outside. Uday closed his eyes in an act of being asleep. She tiptoed near his bed, kept a file by his pillow, kissed him on the forehead, and approached towards the door. Uday held her hand from behind and made her sit on the bed.

"Oh! I thought you had slept," she wondered.

"Maa, I am sorry. I don't want to build my business costing your tears. In fact, all this was to make you happy, to see your smile," Uday apologised.

"I am happy Uday."

"Then I am happy too... I will join another job, no business, no selling of that plot. Okay!"

"No, you have to sell the plot and do the business. In this file you will get all that plot related papers," she ordered pointing at the file.

"But it's hurting you."

"Your disdaining attitude to your father hurt me more. At least this plot will remind you about him, whenever you will achieve any success in your business," she stated sentimentally and left the room on hurried feet.

While dream becomes larger than life

Uday sold the plot, and Adhyayan withdrew all investments of Shristi's from LIC. In the next three months, 'Schoolyard' had a dream takeoff in the sky of success, spreading two long financial wings. Few more schools also joined them inspired by the other schools that benefited from their services. The website featured on the front page of a few of Bangalore's local newspapers. One of the biggest school-office's merchandise retailer, Staples approached them to advertise their Bangalore's outlets on their website. Soon, Schoolyard became a paid-website. They leased an office – one floor with two conference rooms, one cabin, and one pantry and hired few more employees to sustain their budding business.

Adhyayan and Rajasekaran were quite satiated in Schoolyard's success, but Uday wasn't, as still then few eminent schools including Mr. R.V. Gowda's 'Krishna Boy's High School' weren't enrolled under Schoolyard. They had been spending a considerable amount of time since the service had become paid to contrive a fresh program, which could elicit those schools to join them. However, they landed in obscurity each time.

After few more days, Uday called Adhyayan post midnight. He groped for his cell phone by the pillow in the darkness of the bedroom, gnashing in irritation and held the cell phone's screen in front of his face. His eyes shrank impetuously on the sudden flash of light.

"Uday, what's the matter? Its two a.m. man!" he snarled receiving the call.

"Come to the office and pickup Raja on the way. It's very urgent," Uday replied excitedly.

"What..." the call got disconnected before he could complete.

He got off the bed cautiously, wore a T-shirt that his hand found first in that darkness over the shorts; collected the car key and came out of the bedroom tiptoeing and trying not to disturb Shristi's sleep. All lights were off except the one in the conference room, when he reached the office with Rajasekaran. They rushed to the conference room and entered jerking the door hard. They found Uday standing and gazing at the white board on the wall resting his back by the big table. On the left corner on the board the word, 'School' and at the opposite corner the phrase, 'Motive of opting a service' had been written encircled by few scribbling circles. In the middle, the words – Survival Necessity, Improvisation Necessity, Luxury or Show-off, Envy and Jealousy were jotted down in a list format. Uday glanced at them smiling.

"It wasn't funny Uday. I was fucking scared to death," Adhyayan shouted in frustration, panting like a dog in the summer.

"Yes it's not. It's a serious plan for 'Schoolyard' to conquer Bangalore and then India," Uday stated calmly, penning three more words under the word, 'School' – Teacher, parents and students.

"Why the hell do you have to play a prank for that? You could have told the truth," Adhyayan snapped back.

"We wouldn't have come here then, at this time," Rajasekaran said smiling.

"Saala, guru ka chela," Adhyayan murmured in anger.

"Adi, this is not the time to sleep. We have to run a long way, it's just the beginning. Now, relax and watch Uday's night-show, which will be the biggest show of India in the near future," Uday said dramatically, inclining on the table. Adhyayan sat on a chair, and Rajasekaran climbed on the table.

"Our clients are schools, and these are the different motives for a school to adopt a service. Schoolyard is not the kind of service that falls under survival necessity, right? An institution can survive without Schoolyard," Uday started explaining pointing to the board. Adhyayan and Rajasekaran nodded their acceptation.

Uday continued sticking through the words, 'Survival necessity.' "But it falls under these four kinds." He ticked on the words – improvisation necessity, luxury or show-off, envy and jealousy. "But, unfortunately some of the schools are not considering Schoolyard to help in their improvisation, for example Mr. Gowda's school. And luxury or show-off is not a strong motive respect to business. It's applicable for personal matters only... correct?" Uday asked striking through the other two points, 'Improvisation necessity' and 'luxury or show-off.'

"Can we come to the point directly? What are we planning to do? Shall we ask our enrolled schools to provoke others?" Adhyayan asked yawning; boredom was prominent on his face.

"Yessss you got it!" Uday shouted excitedly and continued, "So, we will conduct an online exam for all the classes among all the schools; I mean an interscholastic exam. And the first three ranks given to the students of each class will get a sponsorship for their school-stationery up to the next exam of Schoolyard. Addition to that their picture will be published on our website under a new page, 'Wall of Fame.'"

"Hmmm! So, who will set the question papers?" Rajasekaran asked.

"Teachers, they will be playing the most important role in this plan. We will distribute that responsibility equally among the schools. I mean two subjects of two classes from each school or whatever the count will come. It won't be much burden for them also," Uday explained.

"Uday, we are just settled a bit after a big financial crisis. I don't believe it will be a good plan to reinvest now," said Adhyayan concerned.

"Adi, don't think about settling down now; we have to run a long way. We can't approach the schools out of Bangalore until all of them aren't coming under Schoolyard," said Uday.

"Okay, but let's not go for a yearly unlimited sponsorship...."

Their discussion prolonged till morning until the Plan, 'Wall of Fame' had taken a perfect contour.

The next couple of months evaporated in a symposium regarding 'Wall of Fame' with all the enlisted schools and developing the website to perform as per expectation. Workload had been mounting up by leaps and bounds, especially for Adhyayan. He had to take care of his conceiving wife. Hence, he decided to follow Uday, as he considered his job was paltrier weighing against Schoolyard and Shristi.

That morning, Shristi woke up with a colossal weakness. She tried to creep up from the bed holding her bulging belly cautiously, but gave up being discomfited. She stooped impotently, feeling frail even to carry herself. She closed her eyes in an unendurable pain at all the limbs' junctions. Tears oozed out soaking her wobbly eyelash and dropped on the pillow. She stretched out her hand groping on the bed and poked Adhyayan. Initially, he reacted like a retard, as he was sleepy and panicked, while he got the complete conciseness on the next tick, "Are you okay Shristi? I warned not to get into this. Let's go to the doctor."

"Don't behave like a kid, I am fine. Just... get me those," she fumbled pointing to the hot-water-bags that had fallen on the floor from the bed. Adhyayan jumped out of the bed and brought those as quickly as possible. She placed one under her back and another sandwiched between two thighs.

"Are you feeling good now?" he asked impatiently expecting a 'yes' from her, but she kept eyes closed, mute. He repeated his question.

"Adi, is this a magic show or what?" she snapped back loudly. He quietly sat by her, making a displeasing face. She glanced at him and smiled at his puerility.

"Come, give me a hug! That will absorb aaaall my pain," she invited stretching her hand wide-open, smiling. He wrapped her in his arms affectionately and kissed her on her forehead, eyelids and lips. He lifted her T-shirt, baring her bulged belly and kissed on it, cuddling her.

"Is she moving or kicking?" he asked, placing his ear on her belly and after few seconds of concentration said, "No, she will be a nice, calm, and decent like you as I wish."

"No, he will be a naughty boy like you, as I wish," she said caressing his hair.

After a few moments of silence, she whispered in ambivalences, "Adi, I am scared!"

"Don't worry, I am here with you," he consoled, embracing her adorably.

"I don't think I will be able to tolerate that labour pain. I Googled; it's not so easy. Moreover, you have quit the job, if something goes wrong we might need a lot of money to be in command of that circumstance. It wasn't a witty decision Adi," she expressed her vulnerable state of mind.

"Don't worry; Schoolyard is getting a fantastic response. Next month we are launching a new service of interschool exam.

All the teachers and parents are excited about it. We got sponsorship as well. Everything is well..." His enthusiastic bravado got interrupted by a message-tone on his mobile. "Ok, I have to reach there before 9 a.m. I am going to prepare breakfast for us," Adhyayan informed after reading the message from Uday.

*****

'Wall of Fame' had launched as per the schedule, just one month before the final examination, promising two aids as awards. However, parents had interpreted that service so differently that Uday could never have thought of. Parents had taken it seriously as it had been offering an infrastructure to scrutinize their children's preparation compared to the rest of the students in the town, especially for those, who were about to appear in the board exams. However, 'Wall of Fame' had wedged students negatively, mounting up the pressure to perform their best. They had already been suffocating by the tremendous stress of the educational system. As the last bolt on the coffin 'Wall of Fame' engulfed their left out tiny spare time of daily life. Parents had started treating their children as the gladiators on the bloody battlefields in a belligerence to see them at the top, and they had to preserve their parent's insincere pride. That antagonism had torn out their soft infancy; although most of those adolescents endured that pain, sacrificing the cocoon of pampers, but few got shattered. And one of the students had found eradicating himself as the easiest way to get alleviation, while he failed to keep his parent's expectations.

"Have you seen this Uday?!" Adhyayan thrashed the newspaper on the table in front of Uday and Rajasekaran, and continued, "He was a brilliant student, never stood second in his school, but had failed to come in the first three positions in 'Wall of Fame.'"

Uday and Rajasekaran were busy in a technical discussion on the new page of suggestion in one of the Schoolyard's meeting rooms. Uday threw a glance at the newspaper and said, "What can we do for this? This incident just should have been a lesson learnt for him and his parents that maybe he is the best in his school, but not in the town."

Adhyayan shouted picking the paper from the table, "What kind of lesson are you talking about? Is this a lesson?" He threw it back in disgust and continued, "We have to take this, 'Wall of Fame' down from our website." Rajasekaran held the newspaper and started reading.

"Adi, it's his parents to blame, not us. It's clearly written there; his parents misbehaved with him after the result," Uday excused calmly.

Adhyayan wasn't ready to buy Uday's rationalized answer and snapped back, "Whatever it is. We cannot wash our hands off this. We too are responsible for his suicide."

"Adi is correct. Uday, we should think about it," Rajasekaran uttered lamentably.

"We can't change our policy for a weak person, who can't accept the defeat positively and fight-back," Uday said blankly. After a chilled and discomforting silence Adhyayan left the meeting room abruptly dashing the door shut.

A fresh blood scented old wound

The Bangalore airport was on the outskirts of the city, on top of it the massive departing traffic from offices on an ordinary weekday lengthened their journey to reach home. That tiresome long drive had made Adhyayan exhausted more than the jetlag. He badly wanted to lob himself on the lap of the soft cushion on the bed, but the circumstance wasn't sympathetic to mollycoddle his sluggishness. He called Rajasekaran in a horrific anxiety from Shristi's cell phone.

"Yes Shristi, Adi returned?" Rajasekaran responded on the first partially completed ring.

"Hey Raja, this is Adi. How are you?"

"Oh man! Feeling much better after hearing your voice man!" he exhaled loudly.

"What next, any plan?"

"Yeah, as of now I have arranged a lawyer... appointment at 10:30 a.m., tomorrow," he informed continuing his excitement uninterrupted.

"That's a good move. Okay, drop by my place before that. We need to discuss before that," he said in a subdued and a worn-out voice.

"Sure, take rest. Don't worry Adi, everything will be alright," he assured, consoling himself more than Adhyayan.

Adhyayan hung up the phone and closed his eyes, loosening up his tired body on the couch. Soon he had fallen asleep in pliable cosiness. Eventually, Shristi noticed him sleeping on the sofa, not changed and even with his shoes on. She gazed at his face, smiling pleasantly for a few moments and sat on his lap.

"Oh! Feeling very tired, so slept," he muttered a subdued whisper.

She kissed him on his lips and told, "Go... change, have some food then go to bed." He nodded. She hid her face on his chest, embracing him.

"Let me go! I don't have the strength to lift you up now," he whispered close to her ear and kissed on it.

She mocked adorably, getting up and said, "It needs love, not strength."

"But I could get enough love to lift you, if you stop loving those pizzas, burgers, and all," he teased laughing.

"Are you trying to say, I am fat?" she asked frowning, raising her pointing finger.

"No! But little heavy," he replied grinning. She went to the kitchen abruptly showing-off a childish anger.

The next day in the morning, Adhyayan's sleepy, ajar eyes found Shristi, gazing at him. Her face was so close that he could feel her emanating breath on his face.

"What happened? Why did you wake up so early?" he asked in a lethargic way.

"I didn't sleep," she replied, cradling his face.

"Why?"

"Because the company of my closest man is very transient in my life," she whispered with moist eyes. He pulled her by her waist and kissed her on her forehead. She asked resting her head on his chest, "By the way, how many days you have taken leave for? I haven't seen any return ticket in your inbox."

"Don't know... till this Uday's case is not resolved."

"What do you mean Adi? Why are you doing this again? Last time you resigned, believing that Uday. We lost all our money, flat. I lost my child. Again?" she raised her voice and broke into a cry.

"Come on Shristi, I left 'Schoolyard' because of my wish. Moreover, he literally returned all my invested money; I hadn't accepted it. And do you think it was his fault that we lost our child," he replied wiping her tears.

She shook his hand and whined, "If it's nothing to do with our child, then why did you leave 'Schoolyard'? Can't you do the job with stability? Why are you running away from Bangalore, not even caring about me? Ask yourself Adi. Today you came back for Uday, for Schoolyard, not for me. It's been more than two years that we got married, and still we are living a haphazard life, apart from each other. What about our future? Do I really exist in your life Adi?"

Shristi got up from the bed and left the room in hurried steps, sobbing. Adhyayan grizzled in Shristi's darted question, confoundedly sitting on the bed. He had no answer to solace Shristi as his explanations would have appeared lamer against that impregnable circumstance. But his vindicated heart knew, whatever he had done, he had done for Shristi and their child. He had chosen 'Schoolyard' as an alternative for his rigorous IT job to steal some time from his life for Shristi; though initially it had demanded efforts in terms of capital and time. Even after that student's suicide, he couldn't leave 'Schoolyard' in spite of his personal aversion; just for Shristi and the innocent foetus in her womb, whose one adorable kick used to make Shristi beguiled. However, before 'Schoolyard' could root its branches in the spine of India's educational system, that mishap blew their team apart.

Still that hysteric contorted Shristi's face was vivid in Adhyayan's mind, while she had lurched out of the bathroom holding a bloodstained tissue in her hand. He had taken her to the Doctor; they had been consulting with. According to their doctor, bleeding during pregnancy was common, especially during the first trimester and usually it was not cause for any panic. But, in few cases bleeding could turn as sign of some serious complications. Hence, he had advised them to pursue a check-up to make sure that the baby and the mother are healthy. Her tearful, sceptically staring eyes at the ultrasound's screen, not yet withered. She had been impatiently asking the Doctor, "Is he breathing? He is alright, right?" The doctor couldn't console her. as he hadn't heard that little kid's heartbeat. That incident had plunged Adhyayan in a strange conviction of relating that student's suicide as nemesis of their child's death. He had decided to leave Schoolyard, though that too wasn't easy for him either as Schoolyard was his baby too. Hence, he had reached out to request Uday for the last time to stop 'Wall of Fame' as pursuit resort of atonement. However, after listening to everything from Adhyayan, Uday replied, "Adi, you are in shock now. I know it's quite reasonable for everyone in this circumstance. Go for a long vacation with Shristi, take a break and come back dude, we have a long way to go. It's not the time to look back."

"Then I have to leave," he had said.

"What do you mean? This is a fucking nonsense reason Adi. It's just a coincidence; do you believe in all that bullshit? Move on dude, it was just an accident," Uday tried to console, gripping his shoulder.

Adhyayan shook his hands off and shouted, "Move on!? Do you think it's so easy? You can't feel my pain until you aren't putting off that layer of success from your mind." His high pitched voice had reached the work-floor through the glass wall of the meeting room. Few of the employees peeped through the glasses curiously standing up from their chairs.

Rajasekaran entered the room to control the situation and requested, "Guys, please! Can we take this discussion out of the office?"

"I am sorry guys! I have to be leaving. I am pretty much done with Schoolyard," Adi whispered with glowering moist eyes and approached the exit.

"Do you think, only you have pain in your life?" Uday shouted breaking his inhibited calmness. Adhyayan stopped and turned to him. Uday continued, "You lost a life you have never been with. I lost my father whom I had spent twelve years of my life with. I never can forget those curious faces, gazing eyes, and those snooping whispers from that gathered crowd at my home. I had just returned from school like any ordinary day. I had struggled to make my way through that crowd, pushing them away in my small, scrawny body," Uday's loud utter gradually turned into a whisper losing its intensity and muted.

Couple of minutes passed and no one uttered a single word.

"That cheater, coward, escapee hung himself from the moving fan. He lost everything in his business," Uday intermittently mumbled. "My mother had lain on the floor unconsciously and started keeping sick after that incident. Few of our relatives had offered us shelter and food on an agreement of my mother's slavish job at their home. I had seen her washing dirty utensils and clothes, cleaning those big rooms in her severely broken health, every day, for eleven long years. Though, she managed to wear a smiley mask all the time in front of me, but every night I used to listen to her sobbing," Uday stopped, pondering in emotions. It was rare for Rajasekaran and Adhyayan to see Uday emotionally weak. They stood there as mute spectators.

He continued tightening his jaws after a pause, "Schoolyard is my silent roar to those so called relatives and this society that I am not a coward, I am much more superior to them, and my mother deserves much more affection and respect than what they couldn't afford in their life."

"But Uday, Adi just wants to drop one service of it, not Schoolyard completely," Rajasekaran interfered softly.

"'Wall of Fame' is Schoolyard's USP and because of that service, today almost all the respectable schools are enrolled with us. I am planning to spread Schoolyard outside Bangalore based on that ground. There is no question of looking-back at least due to some bullshit superstitions," Uday replied mulishly.

"Uday, I am talking about karma, not any superstition," Adhyayan burst in anger, gnashing.

Uday smirked dramatically and said, "Where was this karma, when a widow had been dying every day to supply the basic needs of her son. Because of what fucking karma she had been suffering for?"

"Forget about Adi's belief, but what about our social responsibilities. Because of this, one student has died," Rajasekaran explained logically.

"He did not die! He had escaped! He was gutless like my father. He had to die some or the other day," he rejoined and continued after a pause, "I also wish to fall in love with someone, marry someone... want to lead a normal life like you guys. But, I have given up all those wishes just to accomplish this one-desire. And I can't compromise that for another spineless." The complete office was engrossed by a suffocating silence momentarily. "I don't care. I know, how to walk alone," Uday added softly and sat back on the chair.

"Uday, what rubbish!" Rajasekaran uttered irritatingly and rushed down to Uday.

"Bye guys, do well!" Adhyayan left the room. Rajasekaran followed him shouting, "Come on! You guys are behaving like kids."

After a few months of that mishap, Uday had sent a cheque to return all the money Adhyayan had invested on Schoolyard. Uday's impudent demeanour disheartened Adhyayan's thin inclination to join back 'Schoolyard'. He had felt insulted.

Adhyayan's reminiscence got interrupted on Rajasekaran's arrival at his home. He was enamoured, hugging Adhyayan immediately after entering the room. The relief was vivid on his face.

"So, who had complained? And why?" Adhyayan asked lounging on the sofa.

"It's 'Krishna Boy's High School.' According to them, Schoolyard had sold their question papers before the exam to few of the students," Rajasekaran said reading an old newspaper, he brought with him.

"Krishna Boy's High School... as long as I can remember the principal is R. V. Gowda, a real pain in the ass," Adhyayan sighed disappointingly. Rajasekaran nodded, handing over the newspaper to him.

"By the way, why are you referring to the newspaper? Aren't you a part of 'Schoolyard' anymore?" Adhyayan asked agitated by Rajasekaran's behaviour.

"No, I left for the same reason as yours."

Adhyayan closed his eyes, rubbing his face with his palms disappointingly. Their discussion got interrupted on Shristi's arrival with coffee and snacks on a plate. She smiled pleasantly asking Rajasekaran about his whereabouts. Her smile allayed Adhyayan's discomfort a bit, but probationary. Her face was saturnine, and the sensual lips twisted with disdain, while she glanced at Adhyayan. She left the place soon, keeping the tray on the table.

"The police have sealed Schoolyard's office and made the website dormant," Rajasekaran added.

"And that arrogant guy never called me or you; we have to know all this from the newspaper. He might not have my new number, what about Shristi's number, yours. Oh sorry! He is the big shot of Bangalore. It's a prestigious issue for him to ask help from some ordinary people like us," Adhyayan bawled out his sentimental sourness.

"Maybe he is ashamed of his deeds," Rajasekaran justified calmly.

"Whatever it is, I won't involve myself until that supercilious is asking help from me," Adhyayan bewildered.

"Adi, stop this nonsense! You flew here spending so much, on my one voice message; for what? I know, how tuff it is to get an unplanned leave in onshore," Rajasekaran protested. Adhyayan kept quiet.

Rescue Uday

"Sir, except IPC Sec. 378, all other charges are bailable. And Sec.378 is compoundable, so it depends on again," Nandita Sharma, the summoned advocate told the inspector after reading the charge sheet thoroughly. Adhyayan did not have much hope on that pretty, attractive woman, as she was late by almost an hour to reach the police station. And his presumption was confirmed on her first appearance; she must have been habituated to waste most of her time in dressing. Hence, he had been planning internally to replace her by someone who is more dedicated, punctual, and professional.

"What do you mean by 'compoundable'?" Rajasekaran interfered before the inspector could answer.

"Compoundable offences are those offences where, the complainant or victim enters into a compromise and agrees to have charges dropped against the accused," she explained. Rajasekaran threw a glance at Adhyayan impressed on her initial approach. However, she sounded as if she was pouring out a mugged-up portion of a law book to Adhyayan. He turned his face to the inspector blankly.

"Fine, I will call Mr. R. V. Gowda tomorrow. Just request him, if he agrees," the inspector stated in his husky voice.

"What are the charges?" Adhyayan asked. Nandita handed over the bunch of papers stapled together. Rajasekaran tumbled on them as from his chair as Adhyayan held on the table.

The charges were IPC Sec. 378, 415, 469, ITAA Sec.66-B and 63-B. According to that charge sheet, the question-papers were sent via e-mail to some parents as suggestions just before the examination had started at a cost of six thousand rupees for each set. They hopped through the pages impatiently looking for the details of those charges, but had not found any.

"Why so many charges for a single offence and what do they mean?" Rajasekaran quizzed irritatingly.

"This is not incurrence policy that one incident will be covered under one claim. Maybe the offence is one, but it has multiple impacts on the victim," Nandita replied, delicately caressing her stylish hair. The inspector grinned at her reply.

"Can we meet Uday, please?" Adhyayan requested.

"Sure. Rama..." The inspector beckoned one of his subordinates and ordered him to take them to Uday's cell.

After a physical security check, Rama led them through a narrow path leaving the reception like hall, where five police officers were busy attending the public that had come there. The lane ended in a widened blind alley, where they noticed four doors, two at each side. Rama opened the first at the left and asked them to come inside. That depressingly austere room had nothing other than the door that they came in through and an extensive window, covered by a dense iron grill at the opposite side. It was quite a stern penalisation for a person like Uday who could not spend a second nonchalantly, to pass days in that kind of a place without any electronic gadgets or work, though that was a visitor's room, not a real prison cell. Eventually, on Uday's arrival at another side of the window, Rama left the room closing the door from the outside. Rajasekaran and Nandita walked down close to the window.

"Hi Uday, I am Nandita, working on your case," she voluntarily introduced herself after a couple of mute moments.

"Y... yes Uday... She is..," Rajasekaran fumbled accompanied by some stealing glances at Uday. Adhyayan stood at the farthest end, resting his back by the opposite wall.

"One government lawyer was supposed take over my case today. But my luck... he is on vacation and will be returning this weekend," Uday almost whispered. Adhyayan peeked at Uday's shrivelled, gloomy face through the grill in disgust from the distance.

"Raja, I believe he is trying to convey to us, get lost and he can take care of himself. So... can we get our ass off from here?" Adhyayan commented in a loud voice, smirking.

"Please Adi, cool!" Rajasekaran requested and advised Uday, turning his face towards him, "Uday, I don't think we should wait till the weekend. FYI, she has already started working on it, and we have an ETA as well to get bail, tomorrow."

"Thanks, guys. I didn't mean what Adi interpreted," Uday whispered.

"Okay guys, if your melodrama has ended, can we do something productive?" Nandita mocked with a smile and pushed few forms and a pen through the narrow space of the window's grill. Uday filled them as she instructed.

"TC buddy, just one more night," Rajasekaran consoled him. Uday nodded optimistically.

While they had been approaching the door, Uday said from behind, "Adi, I am sorry yaar! Please forgive me."

"Don't, if it's just because I am helping you. Don't you think one year is long enough to say a simple 'sorry'? Don't... until you are feeling it," Adhyayan retorted and left the room abruptly. Nandita followed him. Rajasekaran looked back and gestured to make Uday comfortable before stepping out of that room.

Adhyayan reached the office to meet his manager after dropping Rajasekaran and Nandita to their respective homes. After some formal questions on his whereabouts, his manager wanted to know about his leave plan. However, Adhyayan had no concrete answer for that.

"Look Adi, this is not a joke. Without any prior notice, you came back. Do you have any idea about the impact of it? We have started night-shifts to support our clients at onshore daytime, and that can't be continued in the long run," the manager blabbered breathlessly.

"I can understand. But, I have no idea as of today that when I can join back."

"Okay, I have sent a mail asking about your vacation's end date and I want a reply on that in the next three days. Just minding your performance, I am giving you this chance," he cautioned and before the walk off he added, "Otherwise, I have to replace you."

*****

All charges were quite clear to Rajasekaran after exploring them on Google. In short, those charges were for theft, cheating, harming reputation, sending, or receiving stolen data via computer and copyright infringement. From the erstwhile conversation between Nandita and the inspector, he was confirmed that, except IPC Sec.378 all other charges were compensable. And IPC Sec.378 depended on Mr. R. V. Gowda's leniency on Uday. He closed his eyes in soreness, toppled down on the table hiding his face in folded arms; one question perturbed him, what would be their next step if he rejects their mercy-plea? And in Adhyayan's words 'R.V. Gowda, is a real pain in the ass.' Hence, it was quite confirmed that they might not be possible to persuade Gowda.

After a few moments, he abandoned his forfeited posture abruptly and hopped on the last few pages of the charge sheet where the emails were printed. They were austere emails; the first one was asking to transfer money to Schoolyard's official bank account on a particular date and assured the accuracy of the question papers as last years. And the second one contained an attachment, must be the question papers. In a sudden moment, his eyes fell on the sender's email-id and were glued on it for a few seconds. He rushed his fingers on the keyboard to type, 'Schoolyard' in Google's search-box; two sites floated up at the top, www.schoolyard.com, and www.Scho0lyard. com. The second one was their website. As the domain name, 'schoolyard.com' had already been reserved by the first one; they had to select 'Scho0lyard.com'. And the sender's email-id was 'support@Scho0lyard.com,' just difference in the placement of '0' and 'o' which was barely discernible at least for any parents in normal circumstances.

"Adi, I got a clue! Adi, are you listening to me? Adi?" He started shouting over the phone, hustling from the room's one corner to another in exhilaration.

"Will you allow me to respond?" Adhyayan responded in a fatigued, sleepy voice.

"Oh! Have you seen the emails on that charge-sheet?"

"No, *yaar*! I was tired because of this jetlag and on top of it my manager had given me an ultimatum on leave; so, slept off after coming back home... not in the mood to do anything," Adhyayan gibbered in a clumsy tongue.

"FYI, Uday's bail is confirmed; it doesn't matter whether Gowda agrees or disagrees."

"How?"

"The email-id on the charge-sheet is not Schoolyard's official email-id. Someone used a lookalike email-id just changing the position of '0' and 'o'. So, it's proved Schoolyard is not involved directly, I mean Uday," Rajasekaran informed in a single breath.

"Good! That's a good catch man," Adhyayan exclaimed in a sudden freshened up voice. After a pause, the dullness recaptured his tone, "But the Bank account is Schoolyard's."

"Yes, but if Uday had been involved, he could have used the official email-id right? Why he had to use some other id?" Rajasekaran retorted.

"That doesn't prove his innocence. That different email-id can be intentional to escape."

"Hmmm! But isn't it enough to get bail at least? Rest of the things are based on proof right?" Rajasekaran consoled himself rather asking.

"I don't think so!"

"Adi, I will call you back in few... getting another call." Rajasekaran dropped the call, as he saw Sneha's name flashing on the screen. But it got disconnected before he could accept.

"Shristi!" Adhyayan called in a moderately loud voice, while he noticed the time, 10:30 p.m. He had been sleeping as if dead, since he reached home from the office and had not seen her at home that time too. The obvious thought, she might be at office demised his agony initially, but 10:30 p.m., was too late to be relaxed thinking the same. He got off the bed quickly and started searching through each room, kitchen, bathroom, and balcony; she wasn't anywhere. He called her cell phone, it was switched-off. His intermittent heartbeats were so loud that he could hear them clearly. He had none of her colleague's numbers, while on the other hand she had all the information around him. The compunction of not being conversant about her whereabouts made his eyes moist.

His eyes fell on a glowing sticky note on the refrigerator; few lines had been written on it. He wiped his tearful eyes to clean the blurred vision and read – 'Adi, my intention is not to make you tensed but to know, do you really need me in your life? I love you and can't spend a single moment without you. But it's not about me, it's about us. So, it's important for me to know whether you too feel likewise. I will call you after one month. Don't waste your time in finding me; I am safe at one of my friend's home – Shristi.' He thrust himself on the couch losing fortitude and broke down crying.

*****

"Yes, tell me!" Rajasekaran responded after accepting the call from Sneha.

"*Uff!* Do you know I am trying you for so long? And each time your phone was engaged..." Sneha hollered.

"Yeah, I was discussing a serious matter with Adi..." he answered disappointingly.

"My parents are going wild for my marriage with that business contract. It had been a long time; I am avoiding them; I can't anymore. Did you talk to your parents yet about us?" she asked nervously.

"No... I mean yes. They won't agree for sure," he fumbled.

"What do you mean by no, yes? Sambar, don't make me crazy. Are you serious about our relationship? Do you want to marry me or not?" Sneha snivelled.

"Yes Snega! Do you have any doubt on me? FYI, I am working hard to make them understand indirectly. They are avoiding the topic each time, and they are doing it intentionally. They are pretty much clear what I am trying to say. They are making fun of Bengalis whenever I am at home, saying all Bengalis' eyes are like fish, and they sleep keeping their eyes open like fish... blah blah."

"What do you mean? Do you think Bengalis are fish?" she screamed over the phone. He took the phone away from his ear on an impulse.

"Come on *Misti*! I am not telling that *na*... just... just giving you an example that they understood what I was trying to say," he fumbled.

"Then ask them directly and get the bottom line. My parents have given me one week to return to Kolkata."

"I am scared of their denial *Misti*. I know they won't agree," he uttered monotonously.

"Okay, then what's next?"

"I don't know."

Both of them hushed up for a moment. The sound of Sneha's rapid sobbing breath pricked his mind to an extreme flakiness. He was helpless to console her.

"*Sambar*, I will commit suicide if I can't marry you. I can't marry someone I don't love. Please do something; you have only one week," she whined, crying inconsolably and hung up the phone.

Rajasekaran stood there like a statue.

*****

That was the second night for Uday in that ten by fifteen stinking and cramped concrete box. There were maybe ten or twelve prisoners in that tiny cell; he could not even count all of them, as that gloomy room was not visible completely. But he could feel his feet had touched someone, whenever he had tried to stretch his legs. A faint beam of light peeped through the tiny hole near the ceiling into that living's necropolis.

A warden arrived to serve the wretched food, which could merely satiate four adult's stomachs. Uday crawled to the farthest corner from the gate and shrivelled himself in fright, as he had witnessed that horrific fight for food last night. Few stronger inmates conquered multiple plates, while the others had to starve. Last night's food was still scattered on that dingy floor mixed with blood droplets.

Immediately after the warden threw the food plates into the cell, all the prisoners jumped on those and that animalistic battle for food began. Uday closed his eyes and started screaming in aversion.

Sometimes offence becomes the best defence

The next morning, Adhyayan woke up with an unendurable ache in his neck because of the crooked posture of his head, while he slept on the couch. His stewing over Shristi kept him awake most of the night and just before the dawn his tired body and mind had relinquished; her note was gently halted between his fingers until then. He placed his palm on the neck contorting his face in pain. He left the sofa gently and approached the washbasin, as the situation was not favourable to pamper his fatigue. He wiped his face in a towel after splashing water, took the car-key, and hurried through the stairs to reach the parking lot.

He reached near Shristi's office and parked his car at a distance where the office's main entrance could be observed from, evidently. The car's dashboard showed the time as 5:30 a.m., too early for any employee to reach office. The city was still not awake completely by then. Traffic was still not on the streets, except for few overnight interstate buses, which had been reaching Bangalore one-by-one from different neighbouring states and the cars with flashing L boards from few nearby driving schools. The street lamps were glowing still. Few sweepers were busy converting the early morning's fresh and chilled air, into dusty air, rather than cleaning the street; he pulled the window glasses.

The clock had been ticking away. The traffic had been herding the street as the day proceeded. After four hours of hanging around and observing the office entrance, he couldn't see her.

And he had to leave being disheartened at last on Rajasekaran's call to reach the police station.

"This generation thinks rules and laws are just jokes, and it's so cool to break those. By any means, they just need shortcuts to earn money, and become rich overnight. And for money they don't think twice even to play with some student's career," Mr. R. V. Gowda said despicably, in his known megalomaniac, bigoted attitude to Adhyayan, when he reached the police station.

"Sir, we are extremely sorry. He never had any wrong intention behind Schoolyard," Rajasekaran apologised.

"But it has happened and now he has to face the consequences," he mocked dramatically moving his hands. Adhyayan sat pulling the empty chair by Rajasekaran.

"When they came to me with their insane idea, I refused right away. I knew it from the day one, but not all can judge the future like me. The parents and school's board members pressurized me to opt for this nonsense. We... I mean all the people related to our country's education have devoted their lives to build a firm foundation of our next generations. And these guys just want to upset that equilibrium. 'Schoolyard' is a cancer for our country's future, and we should destroy it before it can grow more," Gowda told the inspector, with a great flamboyance pounding on the table.

"Schoolyard's yearly turnover is one and half crore. So, it's quite illogical that such a profiting corporation will be involved in this kind of nonsensicality to stake their reputation for a pretty small amount, not even a lakh," Nandita stated professionally placing the ledger sheets on the table.

"Hmm, it makes sense," the inspector said, riffling through the ledger. Rajasekaran glanced at Adhyayan with a sigh of relief. The inspector handed over the sheets to Gowda.

"Sir, please give him a chance," said Rajasekaran while Gowda had been reading the ledger, adjusting that thick spectacles on his nose. Nandita leant towards Rajasekaran and whispered to keep quiet. He bent his head down, like a punished student outside the classroom.

"Agreed that Schoolyard is profiting, but that's not proving by any means that, they are innocent. Maybe they just started, in an experimental stage with one school. If they can manage one lakh, selling question papers to some handful of parents, think about the amount if it will spread to all the schools, as it will be more than their current yearly profit. And I believe that's their plan," Gowda sassed, blowing away all their hopes. All of them loomed in silence.

Though, Rajasekaran was quite sceptical regarding his clue of lookalike email id, at last he drew a printout from his bag and tossed it on the table, while Nandita and Adhyayan appeared intimidated by Gowda's indisputable conclusion.

"The mail-id used in this entire incident is not Schoolyard's official email-id. Please have a look Sir," Rajasekaran requested.

Nandita tilted close to Rajasekaran and whispered close to his ear gnashing, "Why the hell did you keep this as a secret? I could have demonstrated this more efficiently."

"I wasn't confident. I had already shared this to Adhyayan, and he wasn't impressed. So I thought..."

Their conversation in hushed voices got interrupted on the inspector's enquiry, "Where is the difference?" Rajasekaran showed the difference between those email ids.

"But the account number mentioned here is Schoolyard's official," the inspector retorted.

"But sir, it proves that Schoolyard is not involved directly; someone else, maybe someone who is a part of the organization is behind all this. It's Schoolyard's responsibility to find that culprit and my client needs some time for that. I am appealing to grant my client's bail to investigate on this," Nandita rejoined professionally.

"I am sorry dear, but I can't compromise, rule is the rule. And I respect Indian laws," Gowda interfered with his irritating glitz of gestures and drama.

"In that case you too should be arrested," Adhyayan, the mute spectator till then, alleged Gowda abandoning his loafed posture of resting his back on the chair and inclining on the table.

"How dare you talk to me like that? Do you know who am I?" Mr. R. V. Gowda yelled, screaming. All the people present in the crowd in the police station glanced at their table.

Adhyayan replied calmly, "Yes Sir, you are the principal of that school, where the question papers had been sold before the examination. Maybe Schoolyard transmitted the question paper to the parents, but who leaked it to Schoolyard. I believe that's you."

"That's not me. Maybe you guys bribed someone to get those," Gowda blabbered nervously.

"As long as I can remember, Uday was taking your name that you have taken money to leak the papers," Adhyayan replied inhibiting a seething anger inside.

"Sir, please cooperate. It will be better if you compromise and allow me to bail Uday. They are accepting their guilt and are taking up the responsibility also to catch the culprit. We all want that only, isn't it?" The inspector tried to convince him.

Finally, Gowda's presumptuousness was softened, and they persuaded him to compromise. They could buy two weeks of time to prove them innocent. The warden brought Uday to the front office, where they were discussing. Gowda and Nandita left after the completion of all formalities. Uday slowly approached towards Adhyayan and started crying like a kid embracing him.

"Please forgive me Adi... Please!" Uday sniffled. Adhyayan hesitatingly patted his back to console him, nervously looking at the people nearby.

"I was wrong... Adi, I can't walk without you guys," Uday whispered in a broken voice.

Adhyayan hugged him tightly and said softly, "I am with you." Gradually, a pleasant smile got prominent on Rajasekaran's face.

*****

"Shristi, Uday got...," Adhyayan shouted after reaching home and muted on the next tick leaving the sentence incomplete. Those empty, dark rooms aggressed like gargantuan devils to quaff him in the world of melancholy. He screamed and collapsed on the floor on his knees. He slowly crawled on the floor, lay down eventually and burst in a loud cry, crouching.

Hunt for the man behind the drape

"So? What's the next step; we have only two weeks in hand?" Adhyayan asked casually flipping the charge sheet, when they gathered at Uday's home the next day morning. They occupied the tea table kept in the garden. Uday had bought that villa surrounded by a garden and swimming pool for his mother. However, his mother had refused leaving their old residence, as she believed that her husband's spirit still lives in that house with her.

"I believe that we should think about the motive of that person first," Rajasekaran thoughtfully stated.

"Obviously money, what's wrong with you?" Adhyayan sassed in irritation tossing the papers on the table.

"Adi, it can be driven by a personal grudge too," Rajasekaran rejoined looking at Adhyayan and turned his face to Uday. Uday was quite lost, gawking at a plant nearby aloofly. He appeared bemused by that grisly experience of the last two nights. Rajasekaran continued pointing to Uday, "And only he can decide that proper motive." On Uday's vacuous silence, Adhyayan called him poking on his hand.

"Yes... Yes, tell me. What...What was the question?" Uday fumbled on his response.

"Do you think anyone in your office has any serious problem with you? I mean... wants to destroy you or Schoolyard... you know driven by any revenge or something like that," Adhyayan asked. Uday nodded denying.

"So, money," Adhyayan sighed. In the meanwhile, Uday's cook arrived with three mugs of coffee and few biscuits. He placed the tray on the table and departed.

"Vishwanath and Ram... Vishwanath handles schoolyard's account; mainly the calculation part and Ram handles money, collecting cheques from me, getting cash from the bank, and distributing the salaries. But they are very trustworthy," Uday muttered slowly.

"We have to suspect everyone, no matter who the person is," Adhyayan said.

"I can't justify both the motives. If it's for money, then why was Schoolyard's official bank account used. And if it's for revenge then why the official email-id had not been used, is still not clear to me," Rajasekaran commented in confusion.

"It wasn't easy to extract money if Schoolyard's account had not been used. It's a familiar bank account to the parents, and they believed readily," Uday justified.

"And the official email-id was a risk to use as it's accessible to all the employees. If, in case, any of the parents reply to these mails, everyone would have known about this," Adhyayan interfered.

"Hmm! Got it! So, question papers had been sold, and money had been received in the bank account. Now, whosoever had this plan, must have access to the account," Rajasekaran analyzed as per the circumstantial convenience.

"Who has access to the account other than you?" Rajasekaran and Adhyayan quizzed in unison optimistically looking at Uday.

"No one."

"What the fuck! Is the money still in the account?" Adhyayan exclaimed in frustration.

"Yes," Uday answered in monosyllables.

"That means it's not a full proof plan at all. It's just to trouble Uday and to destroy Schoolyard's reputation," Adhyayan sassed.

"Hold on! Hold on! We are missing something here. If you look at the mails in the charge sheet carefully, it is clearly written that last year also the papers were sold. Maybe that person got scared this time due to Uday's arrest," Rajasekaran said pointing to that line with his hand and continued, "Why the hell are we thinking that, the person should have access to the account? The account could have been hacked, or the money can be withdrawn by cheque or through an ATM card also. "

"In that case, we need to scrutinize thoroughly every withdrawal transactions from Schoolyard's account," Adhyayan suggested.

"Okay, let's meet, here again, in the evening; in the meanwhile Uday will scan his bank transactions. We have to go to the police station once," Rajasekaran planned with an open question enthusiastically.

"Why?" Uday asked.

"I need those parents' emails and passwords, and from the headers of those received mails we can get the sender's IP address, which can take us to the location of the computer, the mails had been sent from," Rajasekaran unfolded his intention. Adhyayan and Uday exchanged glances accompanied by an impressed expression.

"By the way, how did this Gowda come to know about this?" Adhyayan asked.

"One parent would have bought it. And it was circulated among the students. Definitely, few parents who are serious about their kid's study caught it," Uday offered his self-made logic casually.

They left the garden urgently deserting the coffee mugs and biscuits untouched on the table.

All the parents denied sharing their mail credentials for the obvious reason on the inspector's request over the phone. However, they agreed to send the mail-headers. Rajasekaran guided them on how to get the mail-header by clicking on 'Show original' button in their inbox and managed to inbox twenty of them from different parents.

Adhyayan dropped Rajasekaran to his place and reached Shristi's office. He loitered outside her office for an hour and arrived at the office reception impatiently.

"Excuse me! Could you please call Shristi?" Adhyayan requested the woman present at the reception.

"Your name sir?" that receptionist asked in a typical, trained receptionist tone.

"Adhyayan Roy," he replied irritatingly.

"Please fill up this row sir," she requested placing a giant registry book in front of him on the desk. He scribbled through the row casually and quickly. "You have to fill up her employee number and extension sir," she instructed placing her pointing finger on those two columns.

"I don't know it," he sighed.

"I am sorry sir; I can't call her until you do not provide that information," she apologised in her stereotype tone that sounded like order rather than an apology.

"Come on, I am her husband, and you can't stop me from meeting her," Adhyayan squalled amorally, though he was well cognizant about the corporate security rules. His distressed mind lost all the ethical senses. All the passersby stared at him. Few security guards arrived there in hurried steps and enquired the receptionist.

"Sir, we can't help you. It will be better for you to leave now," the head of security in a blazer advised Adhyayan after hearing everything from the receptionist. Adhyayan left the place, insulted.

*****

Rajasekaran found eight different areas of Bangalore from where those mails had been sent, from parsing those mail-headers. Unfortunately, those locations were far apart from each other. Hence, they weren't adequate to draw any ratiocination. His concentration diverted on his mobile message tone. He tapped the notification to open Sneha's message – 'I have six days more to live my life...L'. He threw his arms on the table before him and hid his face in disappointment.

*****

In the evening, they gathered at Uday's place according to the plan.

"I found something!" Uday said enthusiastically arranging a few printouts of his bank transactions on the table, as soon as Adhyayan and Rajasekaran arrived. He seemed a little healthier than the morning. He marked few of the transactions on those printed pages. They toppled over those pages even before lounging on the chairs properly.

"Look at these four transactions, last year twice and this year once. These three transactions are similar; all are withdrawals, withdrawn by cheque, just three to four days before the examinations and the same amount and all the cheques are in Ram's name," Uday explained marking his finding. After a pause, he sighed disappointingly and said, "I can't believe he can con me; he looks honest, might be a deceptive appearance."

"Logically, he didn't cheat you, as he didn't touch a single rupee of Schoolyard's, just took his earned money out of your account, and maybe the method is wrong. And because of that it had never showed any variance in your overall financial calculation and you had never suspected," Adhyayan commented.

"But still, don't you get a message alert on your mobile? And if no one has access to monitor this account then what kind of calculation that guy does? What's his name? Yes, Vishwanath!" Rajasekaran quizzed surprised unpleasantly.

"I disabled the alert, annoyed at getting notifications of countless emails and messages; I shouldn't have done that. After you guys had left, I was alone to take care of everything and I failed," Uday regretted, bending his head down. Rajasekaran and Adhyayan stood quiet to evade that matter.

"And that guy just does estimation based on the number of students and sponsors at the end of the year and salaries at the months' end," he continued, after a lengthy breath followed by a momentary silence.

After a lengthy discussion, they called the inspector and suggested to interrogate Ram. They had dinner together in a restaurant near Uday's home and left with a lingering relief in their mind until they reached home. Rajasekaran spent the rest of the night with Sneha, discussing about their marriage and consoling each other's crying over the phone. Adhyayan twitchily sought for any clue on Shristi's Facebook profile and failed to find anything until morning except a status – 'Sometimes

I need to walk away, not to make you realize how worthy I am, but for me to understand and acknowledge my self-worth.'

*****

The next morning, they handed over all those printed bank transactions to the investigating officer. However, he refused to arrest Ram after scrutinizing those papers, as all the cheques were issued to Ram, not only Uday's marked cheques.

They had no answer when the inspector asked Uday, "What's special about these cheques and transactions? How will you prove that you didn't issue these cheques and have not received any money from Ram?"

Their amateur psyche missed that perspective, which turned their discovered oasis into a mirage. They returned home dampening the spirits, though the inspector promised them to interrogate Ram, as the course of the investigation.

"Hello," Adhyayan responded, picking up the phone in irritation, while he just reached home and thought of taking a refreshing nap. Initially, he thought of rejecting as the call was from an unsaved number, and he wasn't left out with any patience to tolerate any annoying customer-care representative.

"Hi, this Annu. Can I speak to Adhyayan Roy?" an over-polite female voice asked.

"Yes, speaking," he responded, being ready to chime in her next lengthy proposal on credit card or some other irrelevant offers.

"Hi Adhyayan, I am calling from your HR department. Your project manager moved your profile to bench, and you are not tagged to any project as of now. Please, let me know your preference respect to location, technology, and role. Though I can't promise anything, but I will try to meet them while scheduling your interview for another project," Annu explained in a calm and soothing tone.

"I would like to quit. Could you please help me in the separation process?" Adhyayan asked concealing his seething frustration.

"Well! May I know the reason? You have been working with us for a long time now," she asked.

"That's the reason; I got bored of my Id-card and want to change it."

"Okay, I will send you the detailed procedure," she replied indifferently and hung up the phone.

Adhyayan thrust himself on the bed and passed out closing his eyes.

The quivering ray of hope

They had spent the last couple of hours without any visible signs of progress. So far, every clue they had retrieved had turned out to be a blind alley. They had been losing their future with each tick of the clock. On Adhyayan's message tone, their infertile psychological numbness was interrupted, and they broke their frozen stance. Adhyayan pulled his mobile out of the pocket and opened the inbox hurriedly, seeing Shristi's name in the message notification. He read the message in a single breath – 'Few of my colleagues noticed you at my office's reception. Please don't create any scene at office.' He called her number in a rush; but, it was switched-off then.

"What's the matter?" Uday quizzed observing Adhyayan's discomforting facial expression.

"Shristi left home!" Adhyayan sighed.

"What the fuck! Why? Where is she now? Why didn't you tell us about that?" Uday darted his queries. Rajasekaran was quiet as he had the same question. He gazed at Adhyayan, waiting for his answer. Adhyayan told them the details and added at last, "I didn't want to bother you more in this troubled situation."

"I understand! So, only Raja is somewhat out of trouble amongst us," Uday concluded.

"Correct! The grass is always greener on the other side of the fence," Rajasekaran mocked simpering.

"What do you mean?" Adhyayan asked. "Please! No more unpleasant surprises!" Uday exclaimed.

"Uday has two weeks of time, you have one month and I have five days left to lose her forever," Rajasekaran started in a perceptible voice and finished whispering. His eyes became tearful. He wiped his eyes and slowly stated Sneha's story reminiscing the sweetest part of his life.

"Inter-caste!" Uday re-concluded.

"Not only that, she is different... I mean she has tattoos."

"Where?" Adhyayan and Uday asked in unanimity.

Rajasekaran stared at them and replied annoyed, "Come on guys! She is my girlfriend, and I am thinking of marrying her."

"No, I thought if that can hide in clothes, then no problem should arise," Adhyayan clarified.

"Ditto," Uday caught the easiest available option.

"Listen Raja, go for it, marry her; definitely you will get your parents' acceptance eventually. I have seen lots of incidents like that. We will support you," Adhyayan impelled and patted him on the shoulder. Uday patted on the other in unanimity.

Rajasekaran crouched down, holding his head and whispered after some delay, "I can't, I don't have guts."

In the meanwhile, Uday got a call from the inspector, and he confirmed Ram's non-intervention in that case. In fact, Ram was competent to prove his innocence furnishing a train-ticket and marriage snap that he had been attending a friend's wedding in Chennai on that particular day when the cheque had been transacted. And that transaction had operated in a branch of a Bangalore bank.

"Doesn't the bank ask for any ID Xerox like voter ID or driving licence before delivering the cash to someone? Should they not inspect if it's the same person whose name has been written on the cheque?" Rajasekaran asked naively, while Uday divulged about the inspector's perception on Ram.

"No, they just verify the signature on it," Adhyayan replied in a dull voice.

"Anyone can copy my signature; it's not a big deal. I just write my name. But how did he get the cheque leaf, I keep it in my desk's locker?" Uday self-interrogated. "I used to go to the bathroom or any meeting leaving the key on the desk sometimes, shit!" He continued regretting his negligence after a thoughtful reminiscence.

Rajasekaran discovered that few IP addresses and CC TV footage of that particular bank branch were the only hopes left out for them to catch the man behind the cover up.

The following couple of days were spent visiting all the internet-cafes according to the IP address on those mails. They affiliated a policeman to substantiate the cafe-owners' mutual aid in the investigation. Only one cafe had CC TV that could store only footage of two consecutive days and remaining ones had no surveillance facility at all. They kept registry books just to swindle the law, rather than tracking users' information. The scribbled entries on those books were limpidly unreliable like, 'Shahrukh Khan from lonely planet' etc. Hence, they had to return unrewarded, but the cop managed some bribes from those cafe owners for inappropriately maintaining their registry book.

*****

"I don't have the guts to go against my father. I have never taken any decision in my life on my own, even if it's as small as buying a pen. He stopped talking to me for one week when I shaved my moustache," Rajasekaran justified his reluctance to Sneha.

Sneha had been trying to spur him in all possible ways to face his parents. However, his mental consternation had been overpowering her effort every time. Every night, she had been vowing not to call him again, before hanging up the phone and breaking her vow. Any night if she was late, he called her. For the last few days, they had been trying to find a corner in a circle.

"Really Raja? Then I can assume while you kissed me the first time, you would have taken your father's permission. If he agreed that time, why not now," Sneha replied sarcastically. Rajasekaran kept silent.

"You know how I am from day one, and how is your father from the day you were born. Didn't you know that I am not Tamil?" she whispered huffily. He continued his denseness, mute. She snivelled loudly and impatiently, "Your silence is killing me. Why are you doing this to me?" She burst out crying, began sobbing soon, and disconnected the call. He called his father feeling remorseful about his misdeeds. He held the phone on his ear softly, and could hear the ringing sound, it rang once, twice. His sporadic heartbeat started pounding loudly.

"Hello!" his father responded in a husky voice. He hung up in an impulse reaction and thrashed the phone in frustration.

*****

Everyone's eyes were glued on the screen except Rajasekaran's, while they were scrutinizing the CC TV's footage in the Bank's security room. He looked disturbed, a preoccupied frown. Though, he had never discussed their affair with his parents candidly, but he was quite certain about their reaction, a brutal defiance. Marrying Sneha against his parents emerged a coherent decision to him; predominately his parents would break up all relationship with him, better than letting Sneha die. Rajasekaran turned his face to the screen nervously, while Uday shouted thrill, "Pause! Pause here! Rewind a bit! Yes... yes here." The security head froze the screen as Uday instructed. The inspector and Adhyayan tumbled over it.

"See this guy in blue T-shirt, Ram," Uday said knocking on the screen. The timestamp showed on the screen was ten minute's advance of the cheque transaction's time.

"Hmm, I have to interrogate him strictly now. Though it's not proving anything, but there is something wrong, otherwise why would he have lied?" the inspector self questioned thoughtfully.

On the way back to the police station from the bank, the inspector ordered one of his staff on the phone to bring Ram from his home. He looked frustrated and impatient, while he blabbered to himself tightening and loosening his jaws repeatedly. He yelled at few people impudently on the way for creating pointless anarchy on the road. He reached his table in hurried steps, almost running and lounged on his chair, while the rest of them tagged along and occupied the chairs opposite to him. After few blank glance exchanges in muteness, Ram arrived there. The inspector invited him dramatically to occupy the chair nearest to his. The inspector left his chair, perched on the table in front of Ram, leaned his face as close as possible to Ram's and asked cautiously concealing the seething anger inside, "That day, I asked you decently to tell the truth. Today, I am asking you again the same question, and this is your last chance to vomit the truth. Did you cash that cheque?"

"No Sir I was..." Before he could finish his word, the inspector's firm slap broke his teeth. He muffled his jaws in his palms, contorted, and slowly two teeth spat out oozing blood on the floor.

"Only truth," the inspector admonished, gnashing his teeth.

"Yes, I went to that bank before starting for Chennai," he confessed crying. He took out a handkerchief from his pocket and stifled the wound in his mouth. "I went there for my personal work, not to cash that cheque,' he added.

"Tell me one thing that will prove that whatever you are saying is true. I don't believe you anymore," the inspector yapped slipping down from the table.

"Sir, you can see my bank transaction on that day," he slurred covering his mouth. The white handkerchief turned red gradually soaking the oozed out blood from his mouth.

"That doesn't prove anything," the inspector said returning to his chair.

Ram couldn't prove his innocence by any means and got arrested. However, his culpability was unproven as well.

That magical spark

Though nothing was evidenced then, but a faint flame of hope peeped furtively through the gloomy epoch of their lives. Instead of gathering in Uday's home, Rajasekaran and Adhyayan returned to their respective homes early that evening. Rajasekaran had been concreting his decision in his mind since last night, sassing all the dismay from his internal wimp, still was in infantilism state beneath his parent's superintendence. He called Sneha, but she disconnected. After few more failed attempts he send her a message – '*Misti doi*, if you are ready to spend the rest of your life with your *sambar*, reach Koramangala B.D.A complex at 10 a.m. Love you!' His mobile rang before the next second ended after the message was delivered.

"Really? I am so excited! Isn't it so thrilling to marry against parents, secretly? You are a darling *Sambar*. Ummah!" Sneha blabbered in a single breath, as Rajasekaran received the call.

"Yes, be ready on time, I will come and pick you up. And we need witnesses from your side, so invite few of your friends," he replied numbly, as he was not unanimous with Sneha, but did not want to dishearten Sneha also.

"Aren't you happy?" she enquired realizing his dithery tone.

"I am happy, but nervous too," he replied timidly, thinking of the consequences on their marital life.

"Don't worry sambar! I will handle all the situations and will try to win your parent's heart too," she consoled in a dramatically adorable tone.

He laughed gently on her innocence and replied, "I know; I believe you."

"But, please! Not tomorrow, it's impossible. I need at least one day for preparation. However, it is, But it's my marriage, once in a lifetime," she argued childishly.

"There is nothing to prepare. We will go to the registry office, fill up the forms, sign, and exchange a garland that's it," he said casually ruining all fantasies of Sneha.

"I know," she whispered disheartened and continued after some pause of sigh, "My father promised me to reserve the Salt Lake Stadium for my marriage, as I had liked that stadium the first time he took me there for a Mohan Bagan versus East Bengal football match. I thought that was for me, to make my marriage day unforgettable. But that was flaunting to his rivals. Anyway, I just want to have my breakfast, lunch, dinner with sambar now," Rajasekaran used to run out of words on Sneha's grumbling about her parents.

"But I need one day for manicure, pedicure, facial, eyebrow, upper lips, lower lips and lot of things you won't understand...Yes, I have to rent that bridal dress too," she listed obsessively.

"Do you think those are really needed? I am already two times darker than you; just think about the comments on Facebook, when we upload our marriage picture," he expressed his frustration. She laughed splitting her heart apart.

"And what do you mean by rent a dress? Buy whatever dress you like!" he wondered.

"Pleeeeease! It costs five lakhs, and that's not for rent also," she screamed.

"Then how?" Rajasekaran asked inhibiting his apathy to her insane topic. After all, she was blissful, amused, and rattling after a long time as before as he had been hankering for.

"Maleswaram's Orion mall has a Ritu Kumar's showroom, often I used to shop there, and one of the sales girls became my friend. She will get me that in three thousand bucks for one day," she replied excitedly, and he accompanied by contributing some humming, while he was incongruously scrutinising the Schoolyard's back-end database.

"Are you listening to me?" she asked sentimentally.

"Yes...yes! What about the shop owner? Can't he catch her?" he fumbled keeping the laptop out of sight.

"No, after all the total number does not differing at the end, while they audit the stock. It's difficult to catch one missing piece in that huge lot that too for one day..." she continued.

Rajasekaran clung to her first sentence and ignored the rest brooding in some self-intuition. He interrupted Sneha after a couple of seconds and asked, "Can you repeat, whatever you just said?" Sneha gladly re-narrated the whole scenario feeling exalted at his interest. He regretted how he could miss this suspicion. He pulled the laptop in a hurry, reconfirmed his hunch inspecting Schoolyard's database and interrupted her gleefully, "Snega! You are my sexy genius!"

"So, you do not believe me. Okay, I will show you. Just wait and watch," she disputed childishly.

"I have to meet Uday and Adi ASAP. Bye, will call you tomorrow," he evaded and hung up the call before Sneha could react on anything. He called Adhyayan to reach Uday's home and reached there, riding his bike at a hostile speed of hundred kph. Uday opened the door responding to his impatient, numerous rings on the doorbell.

"We got our man!" Rajasekaran shouted and shook Uday by the shoulder violently, as soon as he opened the door.

"What do you mean?" Uday asked shockingly.

"Let, Adi come; I called him. In the meanwhile open your laptop," he beguiled in enthusiasm and approached Uday's bedroom; Uday tagged along, bewildered. Eventually, Adhyayan arrived there. Coffees were served on Rajasekaran's request.

"What are the similarities between these students and parents, who had been offered the question papers?" Rajasekaran asked relishing a sip of coffee.

"Please keep it simple my Byomkesh," Adhyayan requested dramatically gesturing a namaskar.

"See they all are weak in study, either failed or got destitute marks last year. And by their parent's occupations and designation anyone can estimate their strong financial condition," Rajasekaran explained pointing at the screen.

"Yes, I saw that. Obviously they are a potential market," Uday remarked casually.

"So, our mysterious man has a thorough swot up on Schoolyard's database," Rajasekaran added.

"All technical employees have access to the database and can do that. What's the point?" Uday darted irritatingly. Adhyayan yawned cracking his knuckles lazily.

"But all of them don't collect data from schools. Am I correct?" Rajasekaran asked the curtain raiser. Uday and Adhyayan exchanged glances in amazement.

"Raghavendra Kumar, he collects the data from schools and updates the database manually. He does a data entry job, basically," Uday grumbled.

"My intuition says he goes to all the schools to collect the data and establishes a connection with someone from 'Krishna Boy's High School', who has access to the question papers. The motive is money for both of them," Rajasekaran unfolded his guesstimated story.

"But, we need proof," Uday commented tightening his jaws.

"This guy must have tried few more schools as well not only this 'Krishna Boy's High School'. We can ask them," Adhyayan interfered.

"But planning to commit a crime is not crime. They could just confirm if this guy had approached them or not. That's it," Uday stated thoughtfully.

"Let see first, they might provide us some proof," Rajasekaran insisted optimistically.

The next morning, they conveyed their conclusion to that investigating officer. Agreed upon their decision, the inspector stopped over few other enrolled schools under Schoolyard along with them. However, no one assured anything suspicious about Raghavendra.

"Sir, my gut feelings are strongly pointing to this man," Rajasekaran arrogantly offered, lightly knocking on the table, while they came back to the police station empty handed.

"Sorry, but I am bounded by evidence, proofs. You know we have to be practical," the inspector empathetically responded.

All of them became very silent for few minutes. Eventually, the inspector said, "Ok, I have few other jobs to finish. I will call you in case of any breakthrough," and attempted to leave his chair.

"Sir, can we tap his mobile calls?" Adhyayan asked.

The inspector lounged back to his chair thoughtfully and muttered after a couple of seconds, "Okay, let's try that too!"

Rajasekaran waffled to lend a hand, as Adhyayan and Uday appeared distressed and sulked, while they came out of the police station. He had not left them with any other alternative though, only they could help him in that situation. Adhyayan and Uday were walking ahead of him towards the parking, while he fumbled hesitatingly from behind, "Guys, I... I know this is not the right time. But I have no more time." Both of them turned back to him. Adhyayan walked back to him frowning and gestured to persist, suspecting some dire news.

"Sneha and I are marrying tomorrow. I need your help!" he conveyed in a trembling voice. Adhyayan's contorted face turned into a pleasant smile. Uday reached close to him and embraced him dramatically, spoofing a sobbing act.

"Yeh to khushi ki baat hai pagal. Rulaega kaya?" (*It's pleasurable news. Will you make me cry?*) Uday snivelled in a glitzy quivering tone, holding his face firmly sandwiched between his palms. Adhyayan laughed at Uday's exaggerated reaction, and Rajasekaran stood there perplexed, clumsily.

They turned down Rajasekaran's request to keep the event effortless and petite and spent the rest of the day in shopping and arrangements. Adhyayan and Uday consecrated themselves to make their marriage day hauntingly special. They arranged a bachelor's party at Uday's home that evening as well and were up drinking all night long, besotted. Rajasekaran had to capitulate.

A weird but sweet marriage

Rajasekaran's cell phone had rung and muted for the eighth time in the last thirty minutes. He groped for his phone on the floor dazedly with squinted eyes. He murmured picking it up on the next ring, "Hello."

"Where are you, it's already ten? Raja, it's not funny," Sneha screamed.

His lethargy evaporated in a second. He fumbled, "I... I am on the way, will reach there in another ten... fifteen minutes."

"Why the hell weren't you picking the phone? I was worried. I am trying your number from morning, damn it!" She snivelled howling.

"I am sorry *misti*. Don't worry... I am coming there right away," he consoled.

"You aren't lying, right?" she asked sobbing.

"Misti, do you believe me?" he asked calmly in a low voice and she hummed adorably in concordance. He asked likewise, "Do you think, I love you?" She hummed again. "So, cool down! Close your eyes and wait for ten minutes. When you open your eyes, you will see me standing in front of you," he soothed and hung up the phone affirming her bliss.

He carefully tiptoed through the scattered pizza packets, burnt cigarette butts and scattered ashes from toppled ashtrays, empty beer cans, vodka and water bottles, peanuts on the floor and poked Uday. Uday droned and contorted. Rajasekaran shook his hand and screamed loudly, "Uday, wake up man! We are late." On Uday's agitated response, he moved to Adhyayan helplessly and poked him. Adhyayan woke up in shock after a few nudges.

"Adi, we are late, hurry up!" Rajasekaran screamed and went to the bathroom for a quick shower. Adhyayan tried to wake up Uday and on failing after several attempts; he emptied a jug of water on his face.

Nandita helped them to arrange an appointment at eleven within that short period. They reached B.D.A complex disobeying almost all the signals on the way. Rajasekaran partly opened the door and slipped out of the car, while Adhyayan was looking for an empty parking slot.

"Raja, have you lost it? Can't you wait for the car to stop?" Adhyayan shouted halting the car with a sudden brake. Rajasekaran evaded and ran towards the two-wheeler parking, observing Sneha, waiting frenziedly surrounded by few of her friends. She was smoking worriedly sitting on her parked bike and wore a mop and mow face. He reached her panting and said extending his hand, "Let's go Misti!" She smiled pleasantly gliding down from her scooter and hugged him.

"I told you not to cry! See, you messed up all your makeup," he whispered pulling out the handkerchief from his suite and wiped off the tears. She pouted adorably hiding her face in his chest. Some of Sneha's friends beguiled whistling and clapping. In the meanwhile, Uday and Adhyayan arrived there.

"Sneha, meet Adi, and Uday," Rajasekaran introduced snatching the cigarette from her hand.

"I heard a lot about you. He always talks about you two," Sneha awed smiling. Uday and Adhyayan grinned insanely gluing their eyes on her. She was looking astonishing in a blue sari.

"And she is Sneha, we are about to marry each other in an hour," Rajasekaran extended the introduction in a louder voice, noticing their awkward popeyed expression. Adhyayan and Uday pretended indifferent recognizing Rajasekaran's hint.

"I don't think this is your Ritu Kumar's bridal dress. Is it?" Rajasekaran taunted Sneha, while they all approached the registry office.

"No, it's not. This is my only and favourite sari. Didn't you like it?" Sneha asked pouting adorably.

"Any dress becomes gorgeous when you slip into it," he flirted blinking. Sneha smiled. "No, I mean it!" he added.

"Actually, renting a dress on my own marriage wasn't a good idea. I thought over it later and made up my mind. I want to keep all our marriage clothes safe with me for the rest of my life," Sneha said emotionally, waving the extended part of her sari like wings. Rajasekaran smiled.

Eventually, they entered the registration room on their turn. A gigantic, dusky person welcomed them to take a seat. Rajasekaran and Sneha occupied two of the chairs in front of the table.

He managed to balance himself on that tiny wooden chair fitting his colossal butt partially in it. He sprung the chair by his legs and pulled out few forms from the rack behind.

"Fill up these forms," he instructed throwing them on the table.

"Kung Fu Panda!" Uday whispered close to Adhyayan's ear. Adhyayan gestured to remain quiet.

All Sneha's friends basked relishing the moment through clicking snaps, uploading them on Facebook, cracking circumstantial jokes and misguiding Sneha and Rajasekaran to fill up those lengthy forms.

"Only after one month, you will get your marriage certificate," the officer declared in his gravelly voice, boisterously scratching his underarms and chest. His statement demised that delightful atmosphere in a blink. He continued keeping his fingers busy between his thighs, "As per the rule; a notice should be published one month before the wedding date. But you are Nandita's reference, so I have to do something, though I don't entertain this frequently. I can manage a backdated notice, but it's risky..."

"How much Sir?" Adhyayan probed interrupting him.

"Not much, after all you are Nandita's friends, only five thousand," he pretended grinning.

"Fine Sir, you continue the process; we are arranging the money," Adhyayan assured. Uday and Adhyayan stepped out of the room and approached the roadside's ATM.

"*Ik 'itch guard' bhi le lio bhai, bechare ko zarurat hai,*" (*Take one 'itch guard' also; that poor fellow needs that*) Uday mocked insolently on the way. Adhyayan burst out laughing.

Sneha and Rajasekaran got married on a smooth ride of bribery followed by garland exchanges, sweet distribution, gifts presentation and lots of photo shoots for Facebook. Uday and Adhyayan had arranged a dinner party to surprise the newly married couple at Barbeque Nation. After a long time, they spent the day blissfully. Though each moment Adhyayan had been hankering for Shristi's presence, reminiscing his marriage and a desperate menace had been peering in Uday's mind, they had managed to put on a gratifying smile on the face for the sake of their deserving friend.

"I should consider myself lucky to get you guys as friends," Rajasekaran whispered thoughtfully, looking at the gliding raindrops on the car's window glass on the way to Adhyayan's home.

"Buddy, it's time to be physical not philosophical," Uday commented grinning, turning at the back seat. Sneha pretended innocent concealing her smile, looking at the street.

"Uday, behave yourself! They are juniors after all," Adhyayan bawled out. Uday turned back to the windshield murmuring morosely at Adhyayan.

Adhyayan handed over his flat's key to Sneha dropping them at his home.

"Both of you are coming tomorrow; I will cook for you," Sneha invited standing at the car's window.

"Ok, I will mail Raja all the menus starting from breakfast to dinner," Uday mocked. They all laughed together.

"Adi da, valo kore porichoy holo na aaj. Kaal jomie adda hobe, eso kintu," (*Adi, today we couldn't acquaint properly. Please come tomorrow, we will chitchat for long*) Sneha said smiling amiably.

"See, she is inviting me to my house," Adhyayan complained expressing pseudo crankiness. They laughed in unison. Adhyayan continued, "Just kidding! This is your flat until Shristi comes back. She would have decorated the bed with flowers and all, if she would have been with us today."

Momentarily, all of them ran out of words.

"Adi, don't you find me attractive anymore or what?" Uday teased pouting, touching Adhyayan's shoulder with a feminine posture. Uday succeeded on his intention while all of them burst into laughter. They started for Uday's place bidding the new conjugal a sweet night.

Uday switched off the car's air-conditioner and opened the window glass, while they were on the way back to his home.

"Natural air!" Uday said sighing intensely and lengthily. He stretched out his head and hands outside the car and screamed his heart out, "Adi, this air is like our relations." Adhyayan glimpsed at him and turned back his face on the road, driving. He frowned thinking of Uday's eldritch behaviour in the last few days. He never had seen Uday, twaddling so codswallop or laughing so often, especially while Schoolyard is in jeopardy.

"What's wrong with you? Come inside!" Adhyayan shouted, tugging him inside by his *sherwani*. "Problems are chasing us, please don't invite anymore," he added.

"Your car's A.C is useless without this natural air. As our success and career are meaningless without the people who care about us," Uday thoughtfully muttered.

"Can you come to the point *baba*?" Adhyayan mocked.

"Those two nights in jail, Shristi's departure and Raja's marriage have taught me a lot... altered my psyche. I was wrong. Actually, Schoolyard is meaningless... without You, Raja and Ma," Uday said intermittently with moist eyes. Adhyayan solaced patting him on the shoulder.

He continued, "She has never wanted me to be a heartless celebrity. You know what... her expectation from me was so simple, a decent job, my marriage, and respect for her husband. I am just shooting, keeping my vindictive gun on her weak shoulder. How... selfish I am!" Adhyayan parked the car by the road, put on the hazard light, lit a cigarette, and offered Uday another. Their silence was chirping, resolving all emotional disobedience.

"Don't worry, everything will be fine. See, it has started already through Raja's marriage," Adhyayan whispered placing his arm around Uday's shoulder. Uday quivered in cry and clasped Adhyayan in his arms.

Uday called his mother and apologized for his disdaining attitude to his father.

After a few days, Rajasekaran sent a lengthy message to his father averting to challenge his guts, proclaiming his marriage along with few lines justifying his decision. However, they never responded. Being hovered on their numbness, he called his mother after a couple of days. She picked up the phone after declining on the initial few occasions and whispered his father's strict order, not to communicate with him. She hung up the phone in short, explaining his father's acrimonious percept about his marriage and choice of severance with him.

In contrast, Sneha called her parents and informed about her marriage pricked by a malicious proud feeling. Her parents arrived at Bangalore on the next flight to rescue their business from jeopardy, convincing their adolescent daughter. They applied all their experiences and circumstantial tricks to hone her acquisitiveness for a lavish future along with emotional blackmailing and cross-cultural debate. Still, their effort was proved impotent with respect to Sneha's intense love for Rajasekaran. They had to return empty handed and disappointed at last.

Whatever happens, happens for the good

"Raghu, I haven't got my money yet," an unidentified broken voice complained insolently.

"I have told you this many times before that the money is still in the bank, and there is no way to withdraw that now," another voice replied in irritation.

"How did you do it the last time? Don't try to cheat me! I trusted you because you are from my village."

"Uncle, I am not cheating you. The office is sealed, I can't steal the cheque anymore, try to understand. Before I could complete the withdrawal, the news had spread all over and I panicked," Raghavendra explained.

"I just want my money. I don't care how you will manage. Otherwise, I will inform Sir."

The conversation stopped as one of them hung up the phone. The inspector replayed that recorded conversation the third time, while the trio reached the police station flying on the inspector's call after a couple of weeks.

"Last night, this conversation had been tapped from Raghavendra's mobile," the inspector informed stopping the player. They did high-five and group hugs, grinning, and clapping.

"Hello, Drama Company, hold-on for a second," the inspector disrupted their over-enthusiastic glitz of smugness. They gazed at the inspector abandoning their huddled posture with shrunk faces, deplorably. "This conversation doesn't prove anything. They never mentioned anything that can relate them with this incident. But, yes we can interrogate and strictly," he added.

"Sir, that's nothing for you; still that slapping sound echoes in my ears," Uday continued his clownish behaviour. All of them laughed in unison.

"Or we can create a situation to get his confession," Rajasekaran added. Everyone present in the room turned their curious pairs of eyes towards him and waited for his next statement.

"I...I don't have any readymade plan... have to think guys," he fumbled in jitteriness before the other's restlessness. Everyone laughed sympathizing for him.

*****

Two days later, just before noon Raghavendra's phone rang. "Hello, who is this?" he questioned receiving the call, as the number was not saved in his mobile.

"This is Ram. Can we meet today?" Ram asked.

"Police had arrested you, right? Whose number is this? Where are you calling from?" Raghavendra darted couple of questions becoming panicky as the snow deepened.

"They had to release me because they had no evidence against me. But I have something for you. I know who had stolen the cheques from Uday's cabin and who had sold the question papers," Ram replied.

"What rub...rubbish? Why... why are you telling that to me; inform the police," Raghavendra stammered.

"You know, what I am talking about. I can't explain more, over phone. I am calling you from a telephone booth because they might have tapped my mobile and I believe yours too. So, meet me after an hour at Marthahalli Bridge. And remember, I am the only person, who can rescue you if you cooperate with me," Ram read the piece of paper word-by-word, as written by Adhyayan. The inspector patted Ram on the shoulder after listening to the recorded conversation between Ram and Raghavendra.

"Sir, can I request you to release Ram? Anyway, it's clear now," Uday requested driven by a guilt realization.

"Of course!" the inspector assured.

After spending an hour impatiently, they all started separately for Marthahalli Bridge, a highway junction of four wide roads, always crowded by traffic and one of the areas of Bangalore, which never sleeps. They had chosen that place as that area was convenient for them to hide around. Ram was standing at the footpath by the traffic signal at the middle of the junction. Uday, Adhyayan, and Rajasekaran hid inside a restaurant, where they could watch Ram clearly.

"Where is the inspector?" Adhyayan asked worriedly.

"He went to change his uniform when we started. Uff! He should reach by now, otherwise this whole drama will be ruined," Uday said in distress. In the meanwhile, a *panipuri-wala* arrived with his temporary stall's stuff and towered them hiding himself and Ram from their sight.

"Come on! Who is the fucker now?" Rajasekaran shouted in irritation.

They all came out of the restaurant to keep their eyes on Ram uninterruptedly. All of a sudden, Raghavendra arrived there in a cap and poked Ram from back. His face was covered in unshaved beard, grown in last few days. His tall and black silhouette was vividly visible from distance.

"What's the matter? What evidence you have?" he asked in hushed up voice intolerantly, while Ram turned towards him.

"I have recorded all your conversation with Gowda's assistant," Ram replied.

"Shut the fuck up! How you did that. You can't! I don't believe you," Raghavendra abused in irritation. Ram played a tiny span of his conversation and stooped quickly to leave him speculative about it.

"What do you want?" Raghavendra asked stiffening his jaws in anger.

'Share, fifty-fifty."

"Believe me, I couldn't withdraw any money. They had sealed the office the next day, as the news had spread. I have no money to give you," he hollered.

Ram pulled out a cheque, signed on by Uday and said, "Use this."

"How you got it?" Raghavendra quizzed.

"Stupid, I used to keep his all cheques. How did you do all this with your blunt head?" Ram managed his curiosity as he was instructed.

"Why can't you go and withdraw the money? You don't need to share with me, in that case," Raghavendra suspected.

"I won't take any risk and you don't have any option. You have a chance to escape with fifty percent of the money, if you cooperate with me. Or else, you will be jailed without any money. The choice is yours," Ram delivered the memorized and rehearsed script.

"What the fuck is that?" Raghavendra shouted pointing the micro lens, attached on Ram's chest pocket and started running at hostile speed. The *panipuri-wala* chased him. Uday, Adhyayan, and Rajasekaran followed them running. After a long chase and hustle, they lost Raghavendra in the crowd. The packed traffic on the road helped Raghavendra to hide too. They returned to that footpath and joined Ram.

"What happened?" Uday asked, panting.

"Don't worry we will catch him soon. Everything is recorded now; he can't escape," the inspector assured, removing the towel, he wrapped on his head as the part of the attire of a *panipuri-wala*. They exchanged shocking blank glances with each other.

In a couple of days, the police arrested Raghavendra from his native village at Mangalore. Initially, he snubbed all the accusations and took shelter in a cocoon of numbness to evade the interrogation, but eventually pooped out ceding on the inspector's rigorousness. He regurgitated unfolding all the secrets about how he created the fake Schoolyard's look alike email Id, leaked the question papers bribing Gowda's personal assistant, confined the consumers filtering Schoolyard's database based on low graded students, twinned Uday's locker key referencing the original's impression on a soap, stole cheque leaves in Uday's absence and cashed those forging Uday's signature.

"How did you elude the bank surveillance camera?" the inspector probed.

"I sent another person to the bank," Raghavendra whispered numbly.

Police arrested all his partners in crime including Gowda's personal assistant and released Ram. Mr. Gowda had to withdraw all accusations on Uday reluctantly.

Rajasekaran and Adhyayan resigned from their current jobs and the trio devoted themselves in Schoolyard's refurbishment. They summoned all existing employees of Schoolyard, including Ram. They had to hire new resources as few of them had engaged in other jobs due to insecurity. They altered the page, 'Wall of Fame' to represent the pinnacle students in extra curriculum activities according to Adhyayan. Uday vowed not to take any Schoolyard related decision by his own.

In order to recuperate Schoolyard's benevolence and reputation in the market, they arranged a reopening ceremony of their office. They invited all the principals, handful of influential parents from each school and Mr. Gowda, especially to cut the ribbon as the Guest of honour. They made sure that the incident gets published in Bangalore's newspaper to convey a vivid and candid picture to the guardians, teachers, and the rest of Bangalore. Moreover, they comprehensively accomplished their intention.

In the following couple of weeks, they equipped themselves to inflate Schoolyard out of Bangalore; Mysore was their next target. They scheduled ten meetings with ten different front liner schools of Mysore in the next week. Rajasekaran stayed back to handle all the business operations at Bangalore, while Adhyayan and Uday took up the responsibility to win over Mysore.

"I am tensed! It has been a long while; I am out of touch. *Sambhal lena na yaar (take care friend)*," Uday muttered nervously, closing the file of presentation printouts after boarding the bus. Uday had been riffling through those printouts uncountable times since that evening, while they had been waiting for the bus.

"Don't worry, we have nothing to lose. Bangalore is secured, and Mysore is nonexistent from Schoolyard's perception," Adhyayan allayed snatching the file from his hand. The bus started for Mysore honking, to make a path through crowded

Madiwala road. It seemed as if the entire Bangalore huddled on the road to imbibe the leftover essence of the lingered freedom on Sunday's late evening. Adhyayan took out his mobile from his pocket on responding to its vibration.

"Yes Raja," he said accepting the call.

"Adi, she is in front of us at Belendur Central," Rajasekaran informed excitedly concealing his voice in a low tone.

"I... I am coming there in an hour; try to keep her engaged... in something," Adhyayan fumbled plunging in emotion slumping from the seat.

"What happened?" Uday chimed in curiously.

"But, how Adi?" Rajasekaran probed in apprehension.

"I don't know! Please Raja, you have to do it for me! Please!" he spurred and hung up the call.

"You carry on Uday. I have to meet Shristi. Don't worry, you can do it alone. I will join you there in a day or two," Adhyayan almost whispered noticing their conversation had pricked many of their co-passengers' ears. He stepped out of the bus running. Uday tagged along carrying the luggage. Adhyayan stopped an auto waving and slid inside in a hurry. Uday followed him pushing him at the corner with the language.

"What the fuck! Why the hell did you come down from the bus? Who will attend those meetings?" Adhyayan brawled.

"I will send them mails to postpone," Uday replied casually, turned to the auto driver and screamed, *"Arrey, chalo yaar!"* (*Let's go!*)

"Jana knaha hai? Kanhi bhi chale kya?" (*Where you want to go? Should I go anywhere?*) The driver snapped back sucking the cigarette's butt violently.

"Belendur Central," Adhyayan informed, staring at Uday in sulkiness. The auto started at high speed clanging.

*****

"Now please go, she is going out!" Rajasekaran goaded Sneha after satiating all her inquisitiveness, while Shristi had been approaching the exit accompanied by another woman.

"Have you lost it? We don't know each other. At least give an intro!" Sneha said in low voice gnashing, frowned as Shristi came closer to them. Shristi threw a glance at Sneha, attracted by her anomalous boldness and flaunting attire, while passing them and observed Rajasekaran, standing by her.

"Hey Shristi! How are you?" Rajasekaran called pretending amazed at an unexpected meet. Shristi turned her face back to find him, smiled pleasingly, and walked back to them.

"I am fine! How are you?" she asked pronouncing each word lengthily in a naughty way and probing another question by her eye gesture – 'who is she?'

"Absolutely perfect... BTW she is Snega, my wife," he replied.

"Really! Congratulations to both of you!" She exclaimed blissfully. She introduced her friend to them. In the course of introductions, Shristi learnt that Sneha is a Bengali and their conversations lengthened up over affableness of the same linguistic approach they both shared.

"Okay, we have to move now. I need to be prepared for an important meeting tomorrow morning. Weekend is over, again Monday, Oh God!" Shristi concluded the conversation making a dismayed body language.

Rajasekaran chimed in desperately to delay her departure, "Shristi, Snega needs a favour from you. Frankly, she is shy to seek help on the very first meet." Sneha glanced at him in a clueless awkwardness.

"Come on Sneha, don't be stupid!" Shristi insisted giggling. Sneha blabbered nervously repetitively looking at Rajasekaran for some hint.

Rajasekaran initiated his instant cooked-up excuse to cover her, "Frankly speaking, she has no idea about a sari, but she has to buy one and wear as well at one of my family functions." Sneha nodded affirming him like an obedient kid. Shristi took them to the *Soch*'s outlet at the second floor to select a sari for Sneha. Rajasekaran walked off from the shop in the next few minutes and called Adhyayan, while the three women had steeped into their favourite business.

"Have you reached?" Rajasekaran enquired promptly on Adhyayan's receiving.

"We are at the ground floor. Where is she?" Adhyayan replied panting.

"Come to *Soch* at the second floor," Rajasekaran instructed gesturing Sneha thumbs-up in smugness. Unfortunately, Sneha fleeting inattentiveness in the sari poked Shristi's suspicion and Rajasekaran's gestures on one of the mirrors confirmed her hunch.

"Are you too involved in this plan?" Shristi enquired her friend louring. She pouted innocently shrugging. Sneha's pale face turned red in embarrassment, while Shristi stared at her. Shristi abruptly abandoned the shop and approached the escalator in a hurry. Rajasekaran hovered anxiously following her to the first floor; Sneha and Shristi's friend was tagging long. Adhyayan held Shristi's hand right after she stepped on the first floor. She shook his hand approaching the elevator lobby.

"I am sorry Shristi!" Adhyayan apologised in a louder tone chasing her. She stopped and turned back at a distance. Adhyayan ran close to her and sandwiched her palm between his.

"Adi, please don't create any scene in a public place. We will discuss on it when the proper time comes," Shristi requested soothingly with moist eyes. Uday, Rajasekaran, Sneha and Shristi's friend crowded close by inquisitively, expecting a felicitous conclusion; few passersby dropped by them, out of their snooping characteristics.

"You decided that time frame for me to realize. What's wrong if I realized early. Please come back home!" Adhyayan pleaded.

"It's your habit Adi, to be attended by me all the time, and you are missing it now, that's all. That's not any realization. Any person can fill up that gap on behalf of me," she explained sentimentally precluding the tears conglomerated in her eyes to glide.

"No Shristi, I was alone in the US, you weren't around, but I never felt as miserable as I felt in the last few days. Do you know why? Just because, your perceptions for me mean a lot in my life, and it's all about mental stability, not habit. Yes *Sona*, it does matter... what you think about me!" Adhyayan vindicated gazing at her facile, moist eyes.

"So, you mean to say I am like money in your life. You are happy to keep that in your savings account and don't care until and unless it's not getting robbed," she misinterpreted. Adhyayan ran out of words and stood quiet.

"Any idea what is going on?" Uday poked whispering close to Rajasekaran ears.

"Yes, they are trying to resolve their misunderstandings and complaints," Rajasekaran replied thoughtfully like a versed, aged person.

Uday crackled and said, "Bullshit!" Rajasekaran gazed at him unpleasantly disgusted at his morose comment. "Basically, Adi is trying hard to find a sentence with a single meaning of what he is trying to mean. And unfortunately, Shristi is successfully finding another meaning, exactly the opposite," Uday added crackling.

"Uday, I will laugh after one year on this joke," Rajasekaran said insolently, annoyed.

Adhyayan muffled Shristi's face softly in his palms and perched his forehead on hers. Shristi's warm breath blew on Adhyayan's face. She failed to resist her tears anymore. She felt embarrassed glimpsing the intrusive eyes, glued on them. Still, she didn't interrupt Adhyayan; why would she as she had been yearning for this moment.

Adhyayan snivelled fumbling, "You know, I... I can't express myself properly. All I want to say... I love you and can't live without you. I had been waiting for you at your office entrance since you left home... every day, missing you all the time. And believe me; I felt exactly the same while I used to wait for you outside your home. Please come back home.... Please! Give me a chance *Sona!*" He kissed her on the forehead and continued, "Whatever I did, I did for us... to buy some time for us. Unfortunately, it didn't work. Maybe, my approach was wrong... not the intention."

"This is your last chance Adi; believe me I can't take your aloofness anymore. It hurts; I feel insulted!" Shristi embraced him sobbing.

Uday applauded driven by an impulsive lure in heart. Eventually, the gathered crowd followed Uday along with Rajasekaran, Sneha and Shristi's friend.

*****

In the last one year, Schoolyard had expanded in many cities like Mangalore, Chennai, and Hyderabad and was about to step into Mumbai. They had built a few charitable schools for orphans and street children and appointed retired professionals and employees from different sectors as teachers.

Shristi and Adhyayan had been blessed with twins, a girl and a boy. Uday, Rajasekaran, and Sneha had decided their names, Shraddhya and Adarsh after plenty of debates and research. Adhyayan had worked from home most of the time and used to wait for Shristi at the dinner table with his experimental dishes from YouTube.

Sneha and Rajasekaran had shifted to their new flat at Brookfield. Though, they had failed to win their parents unanimity on their marriage, they had not lost hope yet.

Uday had agreed to marry. Sneha and Shristi had been helping Uday's mother to find an appropriate daughter-in-law and struggling to meet Uday's expectations. Hence, they had not succeeded yet.

21536037R00096

Printed in Great Britain
by Amazon